THE BAKER'S GUIDE TO RISKY RITUALS

SWEET PEA, BOOK ONE

KATHRYN MOON

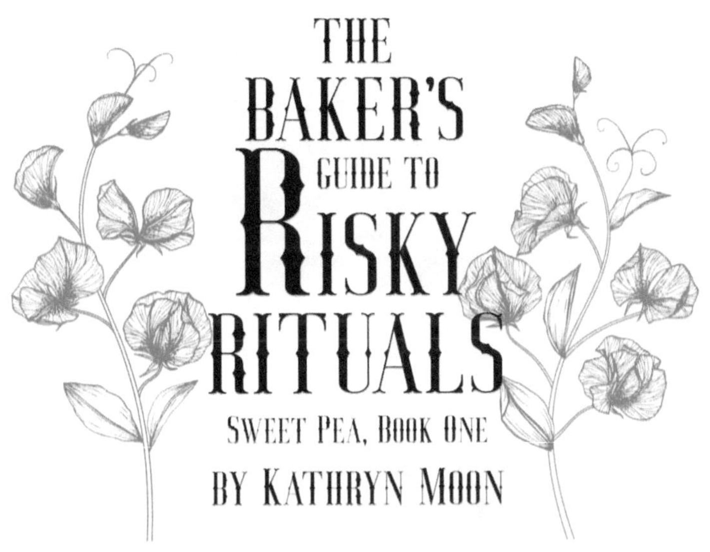

THE BAKER'S GUIDE TO RISKY RITUALS

SWEET PEA, BOOK ONE

BY KATHRYN MOON

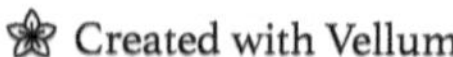 Created with Vellum

CONTENTS

FOREWORD

First, a quick word. The demons you are about to meet are inspired by the demons of the *Ars Goetia* or *Lesser Key of Solomon*, a mid 17th century grimoire of anonymous origin. Some of the incantations have been adapted from the same grimoire, although I shortened them because mid 17th century anonymous authors sure can go on about it.

This series also includes inspiration from Christian mythology, which I have *liberally* and *enthusiastically* adapted to suit my own imagination. Those adaptations, or re-imaginations, will increase throughout the series and include some cases of renaming places or notable figures to help differentiate this story's version from the Bible's.

If you feel yourself troubled by any of those changes, please remember one thing: this is only a work of fiction.

1 KING BELETH COMES TO SWEET PEA

As portents go, the seven riders looked suitably ominous on their black-brushed, chrome, two-wheel chariots as they stirred tornados of fall colors into flight behind them.

The scenery of Sweet Pea was every bit as quaint and tooth-rottingly sweet as they had been warned by headquarters. Even with the sound of their engines tearing through the peaceful Sunday morning of the countryside, the riders received the standard local greeting of hands raised and smiles stretched as they sped by, kicking up dust behind them. The changing colors of the season glowed in the valley, reflecting off the dark leather jackets and polished silver as the bikes rolled down the curling roads towards Sweet Pea, Virgina. The Safest Town in America.

For now.

The threat of the motorcycle crew was larger than noisy Sundays or menacing stares from strangers, and their intent in traveling to Sweet Pea was darker than casting long shadows over dew-brushed cobblestones.

The Hell's Bells Motorcycle Club was a product of the

infinite imaginations of the Seventh Circle and the club's leader, King Beleth of Lucifer's Legions. He led the charge, black hair tied back under a black bandana—nothing fancy, skulls were for those who had to *try* to intimidate you and Beleth hadn't had to *try* at anything in millennia. The six riders at his back called their leader Bell—a name intended to disguise him in the human world. The rest of the Bowels of Hell knew him as Your Lowness, or Beleth the Warlord, one of the Great Demon Kings beneath.

His black eyes spared a glance for the sign growing closer as he rode, pastel paint on cracking wood, carved flowers curling over every corner. Sweet Pea.

The name alone was enough to give Bell a queasy feeling. The pavement took on a sparkle as they reached Main Street, and the sun overhead glowed golden through his shield of dark sunglasses.

What a fuckin' town, he thought, lip curling back in a snarl as a cotton ball of a dog yipped in excitement at their passing.

It was worse than HQ had detailed in the mission description. Red brick houses with pebbled glass windows, and window boxes flooded with herbs and flowers. Bicycles with baskets all lined up together at the corner of a sidewalk, each in a different color. There was a florist shop, peach roses growing wildly over a trellis by the door, and a cafe named Love & Lattes. The rider known as Aim—no King, but a Great Duke and very partial to setting fires— eyed the shop with a hungry interest that implied its arson-free days were now numbered.

The bikes parked in narrow spots designed for motorcy-cles and Bell rose from his seat first, bones cracking as he stretched and glared at his own reflection in the window in front of him. For a demon used to any number of heads and limbs that suited him, a human form was deeply limited. After a week of riding—scattering trouble and chaos behind their wheels—he was already sick of two-legging it.

"Look at this shit, Bell," said one of the riders, boots stomping to the pavement, soot scattering from his footprint. "'S downright hospitable. They got spots for bikes n' shit." Barbatos, although the patch on his leather jacket read Barbie—unironic and the matter of a clerical error on the part of HQ—was an Earl of Hell. As a human he was unwashed but handsome, with a sour expression and tattoos up to his chin.

"Shoulda parked on the sidewalks like those little fuckers," Vine said, glaring at the Schwinns with their bike baskets down the road with a half-hearted intent to disintegrate them. Vine was the redheaded King of Hell—his crown a more recent promotion than Bell's—now demoted to play the part of the Warlord's soldier.

"Not just yet," Beleth said, dark eyes fixing their stare down Main Street. "We're looking at a long stay."

Sweet Pea was the kind of town folks intended to drive through on their way to somewhere else, and then stopped because of how welcoming it looked. And worst of all, according to the report passed to Hell's Bells by the Bowel's research department, the news was that everyone who passed through Sweet Pea had started calling it the dreaded three word name: Heaven on Earth.

Not for long if Hell had to say anything about it, and they had sent their best man to ensure success in battle. It wasn't a matter of Aim setting fire to the library, Vinny bringing in a few destructive storms, or Dante spreading a few good rumors. Bell knew that a town this... *good* started to hold a kind of power in its bones. In the bricks of the buildings and the hearts of the people who inhabited them.

Move too fast and Hell's Bells would be chased right back out the way they'd come, and the town would band together stronger than ever. Real destruction would take patience and art. Exactly what the seven riders had been chosen for.

A door swung open at the demons' right, bells tinkling, and a whiff of butter and vanilla and yeast came wafting out onto the street.

"Oh!" A paper bag hit the sidewalk and a tiny woman with short black hair and glasses almost as big as her face stared with wide nervous eyes at the pack of demons in their best human disguises. "Um... welcome to Sweet Pea," she squeaked out, and then dove for her bag of baked goods and scurried away, head whipping on her shoulder to stare at them again as she rushed down the street.

Aim grinned at her and winked, and her toe caught in a crack, nearly sending her face down onto the sidewalk. Well, that *was* a nice greeting. It boosted a demon's ego to make mortals a little nervous, although one skittish woman wasn't half as rewarding as the frat house they'd left pissing themselves in Pennsylvania.

"I like it here already," Aim announced, inked knuckles cracking as he grinned at the flipping skirt of the retreating woman.

Bell's eye was caught elsewhere, snagged through the window of the bakery on the woman glowering at him from behind the counter. She was tiny, laughably small behind the pastries, and it looked like she had a vicious set of curves on her, although it wasn't quite clear with her arms crossed in front of her like that. Thick, black, feathery lashes drew in around dark eyes, narrowed in suspicion, and her pink lips pursed as she stared at the men. She turned away behind her counter, shaved head of dark hair bobbing as she strode back to the kitchen and the corner of her jaw a *perfect* right angle.

A nervous woman was one thing. A defiant woman was an entirely different kind of treat to Bell's tastes.

"Who's in the mood for a cupcake?" he asked the others. It was time to stretch his legs. Even if there were only two of them.

2 JOSEPHINE'S BAKERY

The bells on the front door of Josephine's Bakery made a strange clanging noise, more like a warning than their usual bright welcome. Josephine Benoit, the owner, stood in the kitchen with her nose to the air as the scent of char cut through the haze of butter and vanilla. Her nose wrinkled as the sound of boots hit the lovely black and pink checkered-tile floor of her patisserie. Burning was never a welcome smell in her kitchen, but when it came from the street it *was* curious. Grabbing a few boxes of macarons, done with their day of rest after being prepared yesterday morning, Josie headed back to her shop front.

In a witch's life, there is always such a thing as *bad vibes*, although in Josie's opinion the term was applied wider than it really needed to be. However, when it came to the men sauntering into Josie's little French bakery, they weren't just bringing the bad vibes with them. They *were* the bad vibes, and they left a bitter, ashy flavor on her tongue.

Worse, she realized, they were ridiculously hot.

She'd heard the bikes roaring up the road, a heady thrill running through her body at the sound, head working up a fantasy of attractive strangers. In a way, she was right. They were attractive, and they were strangers. Josie'd watched them park in front of the shop, each of them tall and broad, sunglasses knocked up to reveal rough and handsome faces. Until one had looked up through the window and caught her eye—the one currently kicking one of her thrift shop chairs around so he could sit sprawled across its seat, his fire red hair gathering sunlight from the front window. It hadn't been spicy attraction she'd seen in his gaze, or even rebellious spirit. Just pure, nasty, mean intent.

Josie wasn't about to stereotype a pack of bikers. She herself wasn't a girl who fit comfortably inside of labels, and she didn't like putting them on other people. But these guys were straight up trouble, and it had nothing to do with their bikes or tattoos or boots.

Her gaze slid to watch another; he had gray blond hair with dark roots and thick black framed glasses and he was eyeing the bells over her door as if they offended him. A gray streak ran through his dark goatee, and he dressed like the rest of them in black leather and denim, little varying details of tattoos on most of the skin she could see. She was about to tell Glasses to back off the bells, it wasn't their fault they didn't like him, when another of the bikers stepped in and blocked her view.

Josie's heart stuttered.

She'd noticed him outside earlier too, and the look they exchanged through the window left her shivering, only this time she was less certain of the cause. He was shoulders and head taller than her, with inky black hair hitting the collar of his leather jacket. Silver streaks shot through the dark hair framing his face, more gray peppering in over the scuff of beard across his jaws. His dark eyes smiled, creases in the corners, but it wasn't a friendly look. More like a predator licking its chops as it spotted prey.

He was painfully handsome, face broad and lips wide, eyes narrow, and his weathered leather jacket fitted to those shoulders with all the care of a lover. His eyes studied Josie until every hair on her body stood on end. She crossed her arms over her chest and lifted her chin, studying him with equal interest as he glanced down at her bakery case and frowned.

"Where are the cupcakes?"

Josie blinked, and it took a moment to shake that whisper soft voice out of her head, like shooing away an affectionate stray cat, knowing it could scratch at any moment.

"This is a patisserie. I don't carry cupcakes." She could give him the spiel she gave to Mrs. Montgomery when the old busybody asked. Cupcakes could be bought at the grocery store for less than a dollar a piece. Josie's wares were baked with techniques that took professional training, if not at least regular and studied practice. Mrs. Montgomery still asked every other visit.

"Three dollars for... what is that?" He asked, sneering at the brightly dyed macarons.

"It's a cookie, but harder to make," Josie said, cocking her hip. His eyes licked at the movement, and the response of her skin was a betrayal, her imagination conjuring warm fingertips stroking up her side and raising goosebumps. She had to stifle her gasp.

"It's a rip off. I could fit two of those in my mouth for one bite," he said.

"For six dollars you could."

He laughed, or coughed, and the flicker of a smile was

twice as dangerous as the redhead's glare from the other side of the room.

"How about I choose for you?" Josie asked. She refused the blush that threatened her cheeks as he looked up, one dark eyebrow raised. *I'm just trying to make business easier with a difficult customer*, she told herself. She wasn't flirting with Mr. Bad News.

"Sure. Give it a shot."

"Take a seat," she answered, raising her own eyebrow.

He cough-laughed again and returned to where his crew had made themselves comfortable, somehow taking up all six of the bakery tables. Only two of them chose to share a table, an odd pair. One with glossy brown skin and a sharp, dark beard, lounging like a lazy cat. The other a twitchy blond with ice blue eyes and unwashed hair. The remaining two were equally intimidating, one as handsome as an old movie star, and the other as rough and enormous as a great grizzly bear.

Josie eyed her pastry case, ignoring the stares of the men, and plated up careful choices. She started with the mean redhead, feeling Mr. Bad News track her with his stare as she served his fellow bikers.

"Canelé," she said, setting down a small rum, custard, and vanilla pastry cylinder in front of a derisive stare. She moved to Glasses next, announcing, "Lemon creme petit fours," and receiving a brief but polite dip of the head.

Madelines for the movie star, and rose pistachio macarons for the bear, which actually earned Josie a smile. A pair of eclairs went to the mismatched set sharing a table. Finally, Josie stopped in front of Mr. Bad News and set down a plate. "And a chocolate croissant for a man who doesn't really like cupcakes anyway," she said, the words coming unbidden on her tongue.

There was already a rustling murmur of enjoyment from the eclairs, and she knew the others would chorus soon enough. There was a reason why Josephine's was the only bakery in Sweet Pea, cupcakes or not. Josie's skills in the kitchen were magical, whether she was working spells or simply whipping expert choux. Her pastries made mouths water and hearts pound, nostalgia stirred up even when it was a flavor or treat her customer had never tried before.

As much as she wanted to watch that experience wash over Mr. Bad News' face, she made herself turn back to her counter. "You can pay when you bring the plates up," she added, pointing over to the bussing station for customers. Not that half of them didn't think it was her job.

Her phone was waiting on the espresso counter, face down, and she glanced between it and the men sitting at the tables, who took slow bites of her food and chewed it as if they were waiting for the arsenic to kick in. She slid her phone into her hand, knowing she didn't want Bad News to see her texting but not understanding why.

Strangers in town, Josie texted to the group chat Rosa had dubbed **what up, witches!** despite multiple attempts on the others' part to change it to anything else.

Babe, strangers are always in town, Rosa answered immediately.

Not like these ones.

Rosa answered with a pack of side-eye emojis, and Josie debated how to explain her instincts. While instincts were generally a common vocabulary amongst witches, the other members of their coven were less easily convinced. June always pressed for facts, and her sister Imogen... well, Imogen hardly ever looked at her phone from what Josie could tell.

Boots squeaked on the tile behind her, and Josie

dropped her phone into her apron pocket and turned around. The tall, lean, unwashed blond was strolling over, plates stacked in his hand. He stared down at the dish bucket, and she could practically hear the debate in his head; to drop the dishes in like an asshole or set them down carefully. Mr. Bad News pulled her attention, arriving at the counter, pressing a bill down with his palm. She started to key in their bill on the old register when the dishes landed softly behind her—Blondie's manners winning out—and Mr. Bad News spoke.

"Keep the change."

Josie was about to say something that probably would have been rude—that unless that was a fifty under his palm, there wasn't going to *be* change. Except then he pulled his hand away, and it *was* a fifty.

So instead she said, "Enjoy your visit to Sweet Pea."

Mr. Bad News smiled again, although it wasn't the sweeter, surprised version she'd drawn out earlier. "Oh, we aren't visitors. We'll be sticking around for awhile. See you around, Cupcake."

Josie frowned as he and the others clomped their way out her door, bells ringing sourly and a last whiff of bitter smoke on the air.

The phone in her pocket rang and she reached for it, Rosa waiting on the line.

"That's totally them," Rosa said as soon as Josie answered.

"Totally them."

"They're hot."

"They smell like..."

"Leather? Sex? Bad decisions? Whiskey?"

Josie frowned, staring past the black clad figures disappearing down the street and over to where Rosa hovered in her front window, black curls a wild mane around her head, dressed in some flowing red sheath or kimono or something.

"You give a lot of thought to the way men smell?" Josie asked.

"When they look like that, I do. C'mon. Bikers. Bad boys. It's like a thing right?"

It was a thing. "They smell like brimstone."

Rosa was silent for a stretch, and Josie could see her staring across the street into her windows, that full red pout of hers pursed tight. "I don't believe you know what brimstone smells like, babe."

"I'm having an instinct."

"Oh, an instinct." Josie honestly couldn't tell if Rosa was being sarcastic or not. "Hey, I see June. Yeah. She's watching them too. Kay, so if they're like, werewolves or some shit, I call dibs on the big hairy one. Or Mr. Glasses. Hellooo, Sid Delicious."

"Werewolves? I think you're getting high on those bouquets of yours," Josie said, laughing and head shaking. She loved all her coven witches, but June and Imogen had too much on their plates most days to remember to laugh, and Josie had to admit that her moods ran more towards prickly than sunshine. Rosa reminded them all to laugh.

"I'm definitely getting high in here. Haven't opened a window in like three weeks. Hmm, Orlando Peabody just met them at the empty store front at the end. They're going inside. June's giving me a look."

"Coven meeting," Josie guessed.

"Coven meeting," Rosa agreed.

Their phones chimed in chorus and with a glance through each other's shop windows, both women hung up to look at the new text in the group chat.

Coven meeting, tonight 10:30.

"Bakery," Josie whispered, crossing her fingers.

Bakery, June texted.

I better be seeing some beignets waiting for me when I walk in that door, Rosa added to the group chat, and Josie grinned.

BEIGNETS WERE NOT on the *Josephine's Bakery* menu. She learned to make them in the Tremé neighborhood of New Orleans with her Mémé—before Ramona Benoit hauled herself and her daughter north to Virginia for a man who didn't want to be chased. There was such a thing as French beignets, made with buttery choux instead of yeasted dough, but Josie preferred to keep Mémé's tradition, and she preferred not to put a price on it. It was good to make beignets for the people you cared about. It was less fun to imagine bagging them up and handing them over to neighbors who bitched about prices behind your back.

Since her guests for the evening were her coven, she went ahead and stretched her magic for the project, stirring up the batter with her favorite wooden spoon, humming along to Nina Simone and thinking sweet thoughts. Good deals on blooms for Rosa's florist shop, and healthy plants in her garden. A snappy winter to drive customers to June's yarn store. Imogen was trickier, and Josie couldn't think of anything the fourth witch in their coven might want aside from privacy. It would have to do.

She rolled the dough out, trimmed the sheet into tidy squares, each step filled with good wishes for her friends. Kitchen magic was humble but effective. Work with love, and then offer it to the people who needed it, that was what Mémé always said.

Josie was flipping the beignets in oil when the back door of the kitchen opened.

"Hey, babe," Rosa called in a strange, gruff and comical voice. "It's yo big, bad, rough and tumble biker man comin' to- oh, wait, hold up."

Shuffling steps stopped in front of the small altar and Josie heard Rosa murmur her hello's to the Benoit family spirits. Ghede Linto and Filomez from Mémé's Haitian Vodou side. It was only a small table altar, a small bowl of rum and pennies, some rough wheat stalk, little figurines. Subtle enough that Josie could tuck it into the corner and keep it tidy. It needed a see-me-not charm when the inspectors came, but it stayed put and she refreshed the offerings everyday. One thing a Benoit woman knew was that you didn't offend the Loa in Vodou. Those spirits didn't come to play.

"Okay, yes hello," Rosa said, sweeping over to the fryer and pressing a lipstick kiss to Josie's cheek.

"Keep your fringe out of the oil," Josie greeted, flicking at the long red strings of Rosa's top that dangled dangerously over the hot fryer.

"The others here yet?"

"No June yet. Never heard from Imogen."

"June probably went to pick her up," Rosa said, shrugging, and watching the progress on the stove with avid interest.

"Imogen has a car and she knows how to get here," Josie said, trying to sound mild and landing more towards tart.

Rosa hummed in agreement, and they shared an understanding without words. Imogen probably wouldn't bother with their little coven at all if it weren't for June's less than gentle nudging.

"Can I put the sugar on?" Rosa asked as Josie started to

lift a basket of sizzling pastry out of oil and onto a paper towel lined tray.

"Go for it. Sifter is just there," she said, nodding to where the sugar and sifter waited on the counter.

The back door was opening again by the time they were plating the beignets and coffee was bubbling in the pot. Josie tried not to look at Rosa when June walked in with Imogen, the sisters like a pair of ghosts with their pale hair and skin. Imogen walked straight to the altar, and June eyed her younger sister with a worried fold between her brows. Which, as far as Josie could tell, was the face June *always* made while looking at Imogen.

The four women had been a coven for almost five years, their anniversary hitting on Yule in December. From what Josie gathered from Rosa, she and June had talked witchcraft for about a year before Josie moved to Sweet Pea, but it wasn't until there were four that the coven started for real. Five years later, and Josie should have felt like she knew these women as well as her own family—better than some members—but that was only true of Rosa. Imogen was private—or disinterested—and June was...guarded, and primarily concerned with Imogen.

"It feels strong, Josie," Imogen murmured, her hands tucked into her pockets as she studied the altar.

"I try."

"How's the one in your apartment?"

"I caught a word with Peabody earlier," June said, cutting through the exchange.

"Wait!" Rosa called out. "No business in the kitchen but Josie's. Let's sit. Grab some plates, Junebug. Imogen you're on coffee."

June's lips pursed but she grabbed a stack of plates, and Josie helped Imogen with the coffee mugs.

"My altar upstairs is nice and juicy," Josie whispered to Imogen. Imogen didn't smile, Josie only ever saw her smiling while they worked magic, but her blue eyes cleared of their usual daydream fog as she nodded in response.

The curtains were down on the shop, and Josie kept the overhead lights turned off, settling on a lamp in the corner to give the room a soft pink glow. Rosa passed beignets out to everyone, and Imogen sucked her finger before picking up the powdered sugar that had fallen onto her plate. June looked at the dessert like she'd never seen one before, but Josie knew in five minutes she'd have devoured them in some secret move no one ever saw take place.

Josie slid a small shaker of cinnamon to Rosa for her coffee, and she turned to June and nodded. "Alright. What's the local gossip?"

"They've paid up front for six months of the corner property. Peabody says they're starting a...motorcycle club?" June said, nose wrinkling.

Rosa nodded. "It's what it sounds like. Sausage fest. With a tax break."

Josie snorted, and Rosa winked at her.

"Right. So a club property, and then a year lease of Grimsby House," June said.

"Grimsby House?" Rosa cackled, head thrown back.

"Those guys?" Josie asked. Grimsby House was a local historical darling, with all the Victorian trimmings the era had put into architecture, and in pastels no less. Josie tried to picture Mr. Bad News sitting in front of one of the Victorian picture windows, and the pieces just refused to go together.

June shrugged. "Apparently."

"Okay... but... what are they?" Josie asked.

"You don't think they're human?" Imogen asked, perking

up in her seat, a dusting of powdered sugar on the tip of her nose, the magic of beignets.

"They smelled funny," Josie said.

"Like *brimstone*," Rosa added.

Imogen's stare whipped to her, the glass green color of her eyes sharpening. "You smelled them too?"

"No, that's what Josie told me on the phone. Not that I think she's an expert on brimstone," she added, raising a dark eyebrow.

Josie ignored June's glances between her and Rosa. They were allowed to have private conversations, weren't they? "Or just bonfire. I dunno. It just wasn't a motorcycle and road smell."

Imogen stared at her sister, and for once June ignored her. "I don't think we should assume anything. But they did have a...presence. We'll keep an eye out. They could be a coven."

Josie frowned and picked at her pastry. Coven was not the impression the bikers gave off. Rosa had felt closer when she said 'werewolves,' but that didn't feel right either. 'Evil' was a bit of a cliché. Josie didn't know that she believed anything was one-hundred percent evil.

Especially not with a smile like Mr. Bad News.

She hushed the thought. "So what are we planning for Samhain? Halloween is just around the corner."

***

Josie sighed as she finally made it up the stairs to her apartment. It was a cozy kind of chilly as she walked in, the windows left open to offer free access to the fall breeze, and the shift in temperature was refreshing after a day spent in a hot kitchen. She left the lights off, toeing off her sneakers by the door and stumbling on numb feet to her bedroom. A shower was in order, or maybe even a nap in the bath, but she had respects to pay first.

When her mother, Ramona, had packed Josie up and driven them north, Josie had only just begun learning the Vodou faith and practices from Mémé. There were years of gaps in her learning as Ramona had taken her from one town to the next, chasing brief jobs and briefer relationships, but Josie had savored her visits back to New Orleans and summers of studying in Mémé's cluttered kitchen.

Her own altar was a low table in front of her tall bedroom window, and Josie settled in front of the spot, legs crossed in her lap. She set a plate of beignets down on a spare few inches of space on the altar, and lit two sticks of incense and the small collection of saints candles. Most of the Loa—the godlike spirits of Vodou—had a corresponding saint, and Josie had always loved the way the religion had found faith in common with the invading Christianity, while still preserving its own figures and flavors. Rosa's family had immigrated from Cuba in the sixties, and settled just a couple towns away from Sweet Pea. Her paternal grandmother's side prayed to the Orisha, who were another collection of the same saints, but inside the religion Santeria.

Josie lit the Saint Philomena candle for Filomez, and added the silver dollar coin she found in her tip jar to the collection of coins she offered the spirit. She took in a long breath, closing her eyes and waiting for the buzz of her thoughts to settle.

"Hello, sister," Josie said, opening her eyes and kissing the smoke floating past her face. "Thank you for the prosperous day."

When she turned to Ghede Linto's side of the altar she

found his figurine—a small, delicate old man with a glossy gold cane—toppled to the side, and she righted it. "I see your warning, Ghede Linto. I've got my eyes on those visitors," she assured him. She lit a gold candle for Ghede Linto, and set a thin clove cigarette burning in an ashtray in offering to him.

The magic she worked with her coven was well outside of the realm of Mémé's Vodou, but that suited Josie. Her family's practices felt private and spiritual, more to do with gratitude and prayer than any serious workings. June and Imogen approached witchcraft like a technical skill, and it fascinated Josie to listen to them negotiate the elements of a spell, like old alchemical scientists. Mémé's works always seemed more like a recipe, improvised to suit her mood and what was available on hand.

"Send my love to Mémé," Josie whispered to her spirits. "And Mama, if she crosses your path."

When the smoke became too thick, she rolled back and groaned as she dragged herself back to standing. Definitely a night for a nap in a warm bath. She'd probably have to set an alarm on her phone just to make sure she didn't stay the night in the water, though.

The smoke lingered around her ankles as she rose, and Josie smiled at her altar. It was good to have the Loa looking after you.

3 — THE CHARMS OF GRIMSBY HOUSE

Some days, Bell wondered if the Devil wasn't a bit of a prankster. Morningstar certainly had an *off* sense of humor, especially when it came to one from the Bowels of Hell—the unaffectionate name for the winding Metropolis of the Underworld where demons ruled and resided. It was not a place where amusement flourished, but the Devil—Morningstar, informally—found ways of keeping the others on their toes. Like this for instance.

Grimsby House was a Painted Lady Victorian. In pastels, no less. Mansard roofs and scrollwork, spindles and knobs, with a wood-worked gargoyle face screaming down from the highest peak to the cluster of demons at the gate. It was every kitschy, sweet trend of Victorian architecture smacked together in a monstrosity of a house.

"It's grotesque," Ashtaroth said, smile barely visible beneath the tangle of his beard. "And I say that as one of the principal influences of the style."

Bell glanced at one of the two demons he trusted on this mission. Ashtaroth had chosen a massive human frame, perhaps to counteract his general air of optimism and obnoxious good humor with pure physical intimidation. Ash was no King of Hell, or even a Great Duke, but he was one of the most determined demons Bell had ever worked with. He puzzled through intricate problems and had the creative mind of an artist. He also lacked the ego of some of the other members of the MC, which was a relief to Bell. Ash would do the work with enthusiasm and not challenge Bell's decisions, a perfect soldier.

"Apparently, it was chosen because it came furnished. A bed and breakfast that went up for auction," Pie said, and Bell and Ash groaned at the thought of what they would find as furniture.

"The outside can't be any worse than what we'll find inside," Dante said, in unnecessary warning.

Bell, who wasn't feeling optimistic, grunted in agreement and unlatched the ironwork gate, hefting a small duffel onto his shoulder.

"I could burn it down," Aim offered. Bell wasn't sure if he was being serious.

"Save it for on the way out," Bell said, and then eyed the bushes surrounding the wrap around front porch. "But the twinkle lights can go."

Vinny spat in the grass and the faint bulbs all popped and blinked to darkness at once. It was an improvement. Not much of one, but Bell would take it.

The key to the front door was a massive old skeleton with a rose wrapped in thorns at the handle that matched the floral arrangement stained glass window. The tumblers made a satisfying thunk in the lock as Bell turned the key in the door and then pushed in.

It could be worse, Bell told himself as he stepped inside. There could have been a great deal *more* pink.

The alarm system beeped as they entered, and Pie

crossed the hall to key in the code as one by one the demons in their black leather boots stepped onto the lush rose colored entry hall carpet.

"We'll take the basement," Aim said, as Barbie lurked at his back. "It's got to be less... all of this."

Bell wasn't sure what kind of accommodations the basement had for anyone to sleep in, but for all he cared Aim and Barbie could spend their nights as bats, hanging from the plumbing. They were a pair of unknowns to him. Aim was all smiles and the constant threat of something being set on fire. Barbie was silent and sour, which would concern Bell if it wasn't clear that Aim spoke for the both of them. He would have Pie keep an eye on them until the mystery of them cleared.

Pie joined him at the center of the entry hall, gazing in the opposite direction over the rim of his thick glasses. King Paimon was reliable, orderly, precise, and an old war friend of Bell's. Bell had made the request to have Pie on the mission specifically, as his second-in-command. Where Bell excelled at finding strategy in foreign environments, Pie would ensure they followed the letter of the laws of Hell.

"There is certainly an emphasis on...comfort," Pie said, eyeing a pair of blue velvet settees.

Bell didn't completely hate the view of the library on his right, but there was *more* velvet, and he wondered if anyone would notice if it became leather.

"Morningstar is having a laugh, or the house was picked for its name," Bell suggested.

"Likely both," Pie agreed.

A spiralling staircase led upstairs, and Ashtaroth took the steps up, floorboards creaking beneath his weight. Vinny followed behind him, lip curling in a snarl as his eyes took in the paintings on the walls featuring bucolic scenes of rustic farming life.

"Do you think Vinny knows any other human facial expressions than the scowl?" Bell muttered to Pie, before following the hall to the left of the stairs back through the house to a palatial kitchen overlooking a dense back garden.

"You know he's a King too, right?" Pie asked, pale eyebrows raising as he followed Bell.

"And?" Bell asked. Yes. He was aware of Vinny's title, and how he earned it; slinking in the depths and grabbing territories from demons while they were storming battlefields and claiming glory for Morningstar.

"I believe he expects some... deference," Pie said.

The kitchen was updated in shades of cream with a vast marble counter. The counter faced a wooden breakfast table, set with a bowl of lemons at the center. The entire property was wholly unsuited to them. Bell opened a tall cupboard to discover it disguised the fridge, which was well stocked with alcohol for their arrival, and he released a sigh.

"Do you think I owe him deference?" Bell asked.

"Of course not. But perhaps some acknowledgement of his status, or offering him measures of authority, may make him more cooperative," Pie said, reaching past Bell to help himself to an unmarked bottle of Pinot Noir. A gift left for him from Morningstar, no doubt.

"I don't want him to cooperate, I want him to *serve*," Bell said.

"Then you may be on the right track, but I suspect there will be growing pains. Curson appointed him specifically."

Bell scoffed. "So be it." Curson was the self-appointed left hand of the Devil, but he was not Morningstar. It was *Morningstar* that chose Bell to lead. Vinny could think what he liked of himself, but until

Bell heard from Morningstar's lips that the newly promoted King deserved it, he would gladly withhold his respect.

Bell looked out the wide windows onto the garden, and watched Dante appear from the back door, face raised to the night air and his back to them. "What do you know about that one?" Bell asked Pie in a quieter tone. With demons you never knew who might be listening in.

"Dantalion is a recent favorite of Morningstar's," Pie answered softly. "A Great Duke. He'd make a good spy or seducer. Shadow arts, that sort of thing."

"Which means we shouldn't trust him," Bell said. Spies were only useful if you had the good sense to never let their observation turn to you.

"This isn't a territory war," Pie said.

"Isn't it? Not amongst our own kind, but we are here to *claim* this land," Bell said. "When missions go south, the reasons are internal. There are unknowns on this team."

"Then I'll make sure they don't stay unknown for long," Pie said, nodding.

Bell was about to leave the kitchen and find himself a bed to land in, when outside Dante turned to face the windows, looking directly through the glass to Bell and jerking his head.

"Do you want me to—?" Pie started.

"I'll handle it," Bell said, finding the connecting door through the kitchen and then outside.

Dante was tense, standing in place on the cobblestone patio, his head cocked as if he was listening to whispers.

"What is it?" Bell asked.

"There was... a flavor in the air as we rode here. I can catch it when the wind is right. I think it's more magic, I want to follow it," Dante said.

Bell frowned and tried to find the whisper, but he hadn't noticed anything on the road up to the house.

"Can I go?" Dante asked.

"I'm coming with you," Bell said, and Dante shrugged.

"Fine by me," he said, turning and heading around the side of the house back to the road.

Vanity wasn't uncommon amongst the Fallen, but Dante excelled at the human form, blending a beauty rivaled by angels with a sensuality better suited to sin. Bell had seen the way the little kitchen witch's eyes at the bakery had lingered on the other demon, although not with the same tension as she'd had when she stared at him. He recalled the bounce of her walk, like she walked on tiptoes to make up for her lack of height, and the sharp corner of her jaw beneath her ear. Bell had never been particularly taken with human beauty, not when a race like his could explore so many forms, but there was an attraction to her that mingled her spirit with her shape. He would find a way of amusing himself with her while he stayed, even if it was only by antagonizing her into more entertaining and biting remarks.

Dante led the way down the quiet neighborhood street to a sign at the end of the road marking a path into the forest. Merryweather Nature Preserve, donated to Banks County by the Merryweather family in 1968. Dante was still sniffing the air like a bloodhound, but it took Bell two park benches down on the path before he stopped, the first prickle of power nibbling at the skin of his arms. Dante glanced back, eyes shining like copper.

"Witch," Bell said, his voice taking on a gravelly growl of a wolf, face grimacing at the crackle of magic on his tongue.

"The one from the bakery?" Dante asked.

Bell hummed in thought. She had been heady enough, the little pastry shop clogged with spice and smoke that had nothing to do with the wares she was selling. This was foreign and unfamiliar but somehow adjacent to the taste of the darkest corners of the Bowels, the secret places where Morningstar left traps for demons instead of the mortal souls.

"No," Dante murmured without waiting for Bell's answer. His shoulders relaxed, and he wandered forward as if the magic in the air didn't rake down his throat like acid. "This is *very* different. It's... it's dark, isn't it?"

"It's not kitchen magic, that's for sure." There was no vanilla and sugar to soften the blade of power in the air here.

Dante stopped, his back to Bell. "Dark magic isn't what we were promised in Sweet Pea, and it's not in the welcome brochure."

"Maybe we have competition," Bell said. It wasn't outside the realm of possibility for Morningstar to send two teams to accomplish the same mission, just to see who came out on top.

"Is it competition if we're out for the same goal?" Dante asked.

"It is if we can't share the spoils of war. Follow the trail."

Dante nodded, jumping off the path and into the undergrowth, steps silent despite the weight of his boots, body poised like a wild cat preparing to pounce. Bell followed him with equal care, watching his spy at work. This wasn't a bad first night, after all. A curious trail of dark magic was a better way to spend an hour than hunting down all the doilies in Grimsby House.

The moon was trying to shine through cloud cover, creating a blanket of blue veined with silver in the sky overhead. Dante led them far off the path, through briars and up a rocky rise in the terrain. The cloak of electric magic never lessened, it coated the branches of the trees and dusted the floor of the forest like pollen.

"Can you tell how old it is?" Bell asked, as his throat tickled, threatening to cough.

"I was just thinking the same thing," Dante whispered back. "It's almost stale in some places. But to be so heavy everywhere and not be recent seems unlikely."

"Depends on how strong the working was," Bell said. What *was* curious was how this heavy coating of dark magic didn't seem to diminish the glow of the nearby town.

Up at the top of the rise an engine purred and gravel crunched. Dante and Bell stopped still, just high enough to peer over the edge as headlights glowed bright, illuminating a drive above them and a dark cabin tucked into the trees. A growl trembled in Dante's throat as the car passed them, two women in the front seats, a bright net of safety cast over the vehicle and beneath that, a shadowy glow.

Bell hushed the other demon, their eyes fixed to the car and gleaming blood red in the brake lights.

Three witches in one little town, dark magic in the woods. The brief Bell had received had been seriously lacking on the significant details.

A light above the cabin door flicked on, detecting motion, and one car door shut softly. The woman was tall and slim, with hair an indiscernible shade running down her back in waves to her waist. The car made a soft circle in the drive, and Dante and Bell both stood proudly in the headlights, invisible to the driver's eye with as little effort as willing it so. But the witch walking up the steps to the cabin turned, eyes fixing to where the demons stood. It was impossible to tell from their distance whether or not she saw them, but Bell felt her stare on his chest like a hand trying to push him back.

"It's hers," Dante breathed. "The magic in the woods."

"You can tell from here?" Bell asked.

"It's hers," Dante repeated.

"What do you want to do? Follow her into the cabin?" Bell asked, just to see what he would say. Dante was nearly vibrating with tension, eyes flickering with fire as his stare fixed on the witch. This wasn't caution at an unfamiliar enemy. This was recognition.

The woman lost interest in staring into the woods, and Bell suspected she'd felt their presence rather than actually spotted them. She unlocked the front door and slid inside, never turning a light on, although he caught her shadow passing a large window.

"I want to go unpack," Dante said, turning and clomping back down the hill, making no effort to quiet his steps on his way out.

Bell followed him, content to know that his spy was keeping secrets, and those secrets could be dug up if Bell looked in the right places. The witch wasn't an ally, no matter what kind of shadow she was casting in the woods. Not if she was keeping company with the other one in the car, who was all brightness and sharp edges and delicate threads of power. Three witches of notable power in one town was an interesting twist to the challenge of the mission, Bell thought. It would certainly make things entertaining.

4 

KNITTING KNAVES

The 'club house' HQ had rented for the mission was about as qualified for a motorcycle crew's needs as Grimsby House was for demons. This aside, Ashtaroth hadn't complained about the ensuite room he'd snagged for himself, claw foot tub included. He liked a big form as a human. Which meant he needed a big tub.

"Smells like diapers and bad whiskey in here," Vinny spat out.

King of Hell or not, Vinny was about two inches from Ash's last nerve. If the other demon missed the Bowels so much, Ash was more than happy to send him right back there.

"So clean," Ash muttered back.

"He's not wrong," Bell said at Ash's back, frowning at the dense burgundy carpet under their boots. Bell looked at his friend, some of Vinny's frustration reflected in his black gaze. "Illusions or elbow grease?"

"Illusions won't save our sense of smell," Aim chimed in. He tossed a felt coaster into the air and watched it promptly burn in a great gust of fire, ashes floating demurely down into the carpet, before he ground it in under his boot. Ash snorted at the display and Aim grinned at him, white smile shining brightly against his deep brown skin.

"By law, we reserve any tricks for our actual work," Paimon said, examining the shabby bar and scuffed pool tables over the top of his round glasses.

"Elbow grease it is," Bell said, a sound escaping him that would've been a sigh from any other demon, hand reaching up to comb through silver brushed black hair. "Ash..." He glanced over and then went back to sneering at the space.

Ash didn't blame him, the place was pretty bleak. The real estate agent had cheerfully informed them that the small hall had once housed a Loyal Order of the Moose organization, until the senior citizen population of the town was too low to support the rent. The lighting was all low hanging stained glass lamps, and the room was furnished in more burgundy suede, rubbed bare and discolored with age. While Ash would refuse to say the words aloud if pressed, Vinny was right. The vibe of the place was a lot less 'sell your soul to darkness,' and a lot more 'please call Hospice.'

"I'll head to the hardware store," Ash said. It was going to take a lot more than hammers and nails to make the place tolerable, but handiwork was a specialty of the large demon's.

"Keep an eye out for any potential recruits," Pie said.

Ash nodded and gestured to the room. "You wanna get a head start? Tear out that fucking carpeting."

"Just burn the shithole down," Vinny echoed.

Aim shot up from where he'd been hunched over the bar, absently chipping at the enamel finish.

"Don't," Bell barked at Aim. "No serious fires... yet."

Disregarding Paimon's warning about their powers, Ash conjured himself a pair of sunglasses and slid them on as he stepped outside. The sun was shining, and there was something about the town that he would've sworn made that shine *brighter* here, all the colors on Main Street more vivid. He'd served missions like this before, dismantling little towns around the world, but never one that had the glow of Sweet Pea. What had taken HQ so long in bringing them here? The roots were going to be deep on this one.

Down the block from their new club was the local bar, still closed for the day. Hell's Bells would be making a trip there soon to see what shook loose. There had to be at least a few elements in the local scene that would prove corruptible to the cause. The first footholds would be the most important. Dante would clean himself up, check out the political scene, while Vinny and Pie would find the passions that might be turned in darker directions. Aim and Barbie would hunt down the rebellious youth and souls at the edge of decisions.

But first, they needed what looked like a halfway believable house of operations for the motorcycle club. The hardware store, a double wide storefront with the family name of Randall's on the sign, was across the street. And right next door to it, facing Ash, was a smaller shop by the name of Knots and Knittery. He crossed the road, eyeing the window display of elaborately macraméd cording around antlers and driftwood. In the floor of the window were baskets of yarn in rich autumnal colors.

To the mortal eye it looked like a trendy little craft boutique advertisement. To a demon's eye every item was built from sigils of protection, prosperity, guarding, and quiet.

I could use something to keep my hands busy, Ash thought, approaching the grand old door and its lion's head knob.

The witch's knotted wards resisted his entrance at first,

tangling around him like a cobweb, but he thrummed power in their direction, mimicking the snag and snap of the magic. The latch gave, hinges creaking as he stepped inside. There were no bells to mark his arrival as Ash stepped into the cozy space. Sunlight netted through the window but the space was bright with daylight from a long skylight on the high ceiling. The shop was still and quiet and *clean*. No glow of Sweet Pea's goodness, no buzz of a kitchen witch vibrating with tension. Just peace and wool and quiet.

"Can I help you find anything?"

He'd almost forgotten to expect to find anyone until she spoke. The witch was tall—although still half a head shorter than him—and pale, with an expression that was somewhere between startled and glaring. Despite the almost colorless blonde of her hair and the soft shade of gray in her eyes, she blended into the rich colors of wooden shelves laden with vibrant hanks of yarn behind her.

"Looking for a gift card?" she asked, eyebrow raising. Her voice was lower than he expected, and warmer too, and he liked the sound of it in his ears.

"I need a project," Ash said, turning in a circle to take in her stock. The shop smelled of wool, hints of musty silk and alpaca in the background. When he faced her again, she was carefully blank. "Maybe a sweater. Didn't bring one with me."

She blinked and then her eyes trailed over him. *Vanity.* That was the feeling, the faint urge to puff his chest under her perusal. It faded slightly as a frown formed on her lips. *Lips the shade of an overripe peach.* There was more color to her the longer he stared.

"I'm going to have a pretty limited selection for you to

choose from, given how much yardage you'll need. Unless you want to fill out a special order."

"I'll take a look around," Ash said, grinning.

Her hands slid behind her back, and there was a soft spike of magic on the air, although he couldn't catch the flavor. "Of course. Call if you have any questions."

"Who am I calling for?" he asked as she turned, ready to head for a desk at the far end of the room.

She paused, lips pursing, and eyed her window wards as if they'd betrayed her. She knew Ash was off, that he shouldn't have been let inside her safe space here, she just didn't know how yet, and he enjoyed her frustration.

"June."

"Ash," he offered in introduction, but was ignored.

If there was ever a demon who liked a long project, and an intricate puzzle to solve, it was Ashtaroth. He may not have had titles or dozens of legions serving him, but that was only because he enjoyed his humble work. He suspected here in Sweet Pea, this woman might be that work —diamond hard and secretive and cold—and he relished the challenge ahead of him.

He hunted the shelves. June, stitch witch, had coated her shop in artful magic, worked into every project that sat on display. It was impressive and... Ash paused in front of a lace shawl draped over a hanger, and felt the bite of the warning in the work. The amount of warding and protection surrounding the small space was curious. Was she afraid of something? Protecting herself? The front door opened as Ash found a shelf loaded with local wool, rustic and a bit rough, and silky with the natural lanolin.

"June? June are you- ah, there you are!" A woman called out behind him with a voice that spoke of minivans and bake sales.

Ash smirked at the yarn in front of him. So June had herself warded to avoid notice too. And it had worked on him. Even more impressive.

"Sheriff Nolan, how can I help you?"

Ash glanced over his shoulder, surprised to find that the soccer mom was in a Sheriff's uniform. When she gave him an uneasy glance in return, he focused back on the yarn, catching a shade that was roughly the color of June's gray eyes and counting the hanks. The stitch witch was right. He was big and it was going to take a lot of yarn to make a sweater to fit his massive frame, but she had a good stock and it had been a long time since he'd gotten to work with human hands.

"It's a… it's just a funny little local thing but I uh… I thought you might be able to…umm…" Footsteps shuffled farther away from Ash, and voices lowered. "It's just that some campers came into the station this morning after, well, *seeing some things* out in the woods."

Quiet followed, and Sheriff Nolan cleared her throat several times before speaking again when June refused to. "Um, some symbols and…tools and things. Some blood too," she added softly. "Not that I think you or- well not that I think you know anything about it. Just that you might be able to say whether or not it was just teenagers or…"

"I see." June's voice clipped around the soft words. "Where in the woods?"

"Near the main campsites. Rangers say some new campers are expected this afternoon—"

"I can take a look after work, but I have the shop to run until five, Sheriff."

Ash turned his face away so they couldn't catch him grinning. She was a mean little stitch witch, and tough as steel. *Incorruptible*, he thought. It would be fun to wear her down.

"Yes, of course, I'll let the Rangers know. They can...keep it out of the way for the campers. Will you call the station and let me know what you think?"

"Of course. I'm sure it's like you said, some kind of prank."

The Sheriff left after a few more murmured words, and Ash tried to curl a tendril of power in June's direction to see if he could catch a chink in the wholesome armor. Instead, he hit a cold and mirroring wall. One glance at June, her eyes glaring into his, and he drew back with a wink and a smile.

"Found what I'd like," Ash said, drawing the shelf's worth of gray wool and catching a set of needles out of a basket and into his arms, carrying it toward the desk.

June swallowed, a flash of mourning streaking across her face, like she was already missing the loss of her stock. No wonder she had so many wards up, if she barely even wanted customers.

"Do you need help finding a pattern?"

"Oh, I know my way around a sweater," he said. "And I'll come in if I have any questions."

June 'hmm'd in response, eyes on the yarn he dropped onto the desk. Ash thought he might even make questions up, see if he could ruffle her glass feathers, or find a weak spot in the armor she clearly loved to build. She glanced at him after delivering the total, a number she expected to warrant shock, but he was on Hell's dime—and if there was one thing Morningstar didn't skimp on, it was paying the staff. He passed her a heavy gold card, warm to the touch, and eyed the contrast in their hands. She had long, thin fingers and smooth skin that he wanted to take between his lips and see if it was as cold as she tried to appear. His hands were twice the size of hers, chipped with scars, and dark with the illusion of a sun he'd been dreaming of for over a century.

"Enjoy your work," she said, passing him a bag heavy with wool.

This time Ash skimmed the back of her hand with calloused fingers, watched her grip tighten around the twine handles of the bag before pulling away, leaving him to catch it before it hit the floor.

"Nice shop you have here," he said, grinning, watching her grind her teeth and clench her fist at her side. Her other hand rose to her throat, some protective instinct responding to being caught in the sight lines of a predator. There was a flash of regret in his gut—an old side effect of the conquering game that he'd forgotten—and he kicked it aside, adding before he left, "Good luck in the woods."

He made it nearly to the door before magic sliced a line up his spine. Ash grunted at the sting of pain, feet stumbling in response to her all but shoving him out. The grunt softened into a laugh, and the sting followed him out onto the sidewalk and even into the hardware store.

June the stitch witch.

I like her. Ash paused in front of some reclaimed wood and frowned at the thought. He liked the witch the way a fox liked spotting a mother rabbit coming out of its warren. *She's a challenge,* he assured himself. Or was she challenging?

He let the hardware shop clerk—a kid with black hair hanging in his eyes and a nervous shift of his feet—interrupt his musing, and he started to rattle off an order of supplies for the club. It was time to think like Pie. Do the right things in the right order, starting with the club. And maybe with swinging by the campgrounds to see what Sheriff Nolan was whispering about.

You could throw June off. Give her something to worry about.

"Color preference on the paint?"

Ash cleared his throat, and reached to grab a handful of charcoal and bruise green paint chips.

"It'll come out darker than it looks here," the kid, Danny by the name tag, squeaked at him.

"I'm aware," Ash answered, the snarl in his voice coming out unbidden.

Maybe he would wait to tell Beleth about the woods. Catch it before the rangers cleaned things up, but after June had a chance to investigate. If he wanted to snare her, he'd have to find a way of getting her guard to lower first.

An hour later, Beleth frowned at the sack of yarn Ash set by the door as he returned to the club, but the darkness on his face sharpened to expectation as Ash stepped aside to reveal the young hardware clerk behind him, loaded down with supplies. Work stopped in the club. Aim and Barbie had gone shirtless, baring skin patterned with tattoos as they tore up the old carpet. Vinny and Pie were dismantling the lamps above the bar, and Vinny paused to sneer at the kid in the doorway.

"Just drop the stuff on the tables," Ash said, heaving a paint can up on the bar. "Boys, this is Danny. He rides a Yamaha."

Beleth grinned at Ash, and then stepped into Danny's path before the kid could make it back to the door and escape. "Welcome to Hell's Bells MC. I'm Bell."

Danny released a soft squeak, the sound of air escaping a balloon.

"Don't mind the smell," Aim added, grinning.

5 BLOOD ON THE BLADE

Josie was carrying out the trash after closing the shop —looking forward to getting up to her apartment in time to cook something fancier than a grilled cheese, and binge some Great British Baking Show—when a shadow slid up the length of the alley. Her heart seized in her chest, body vibrating and feet stumbling backwards to pin herself against the wall.

And then June appeared, stepping under the fall of the flickering alley lamp, her eyes as wide and startled, as if it was Josie sneaking up on her rather than the other way around.

"Ah merde! June! What the—"

"Are you busy?"

Josie blinked, her mouth hanging open. "Uh. Yeah. I need to go to the emergency room because you gave me a *heart attack.* What are you doing out here?"

"I need your help," June said, eyes wincing as if the words cost her.

Come to think of it, Josie'd never heard those words

from June's mouth before. Not in that order. She set her hand over her heart as if to slow the wild beating in her chest and released a long breath. It was dark in the alley, surrounded by brick buildings, but the sun wouldn't be down quite yet. A fancy dinner would probably be out of the question if June needed a favor. That was okay, Josie actually loved grilled cheese, even if it had become a too frequent staple in her diet.

"Alright. Just let me lock up." Josie threw the trash into the dumpster, and locked the backdoor after glancing inside one last time to be sure she hadn't forgotten to turn anything off or put any dairy away. June had her arms wrapped around her waist as Josie faced her. "You could've texted," Josie said, trying not to sound too prickly.

June shrugged. "I didn't think of it. And you're just down the alley. Come on. We're going up to Merryweather."

"Aww, the park? June, it'll be dark by the time we get there."

"That's for the best. I'll drive."

Josie followed June down the alley with slow steps. "I should go grab a sweater or something."

"I've got sweaters in the car."

Of course she did. June was simultaneously the coziest person Josie knew, as well as the chilliest in demeanor. But she was no-bullshit, and supportive in her own way, and she'd given Josie every piece of advice needed to fight the local council in getting the patisserie cleared with all of its regulations.

June's old Toyota was parked behind her yarn store, and sure enough, there was a pile of sweaters and scarves tossed into the backseat. Josie slid into the passenger's seat and twisted around to rifle through the selection as June started up the engine. She found a plain and exceptionally soft pink sweatshirt style and pulled it on over her head before buckling in. June glanced at her out of the corner of her eye.

"You can keep that one. Pink's not my color." Pink would look wonderful on June with all her pale wintery coloring, but Josie'd never seen her wear anything other than soft earth tones, like she was constantly trying to blend in to an office wall. "Just don't throw it in the machine. It's a cashmere blend." Josie stroked her hands over the sleeves, enjoying the kitten soft texture as June chewed on her lip. "Maybe just bring it to me when you need it washed."

Josie snorted, and June startled in her seat as if she missed the joke. The car turned out onto Main Street and headed out of downtown Sweet Pea, passing the last door on the corner where light was creeping out from behind windows blacked out with newspaper. Even from inside the car, Josie could hear the blare of droning rock music coming from inside the motorcycle club's new headquarters.

"One of them came into the shop today."

"Mr. Bad News?" Josie asked, immediately swiveling to face June. When she frowned in confusion, Josie explained, "Tall, studly tower of a man? Black hair to here," she said, gesturing to her chin.

June shook her head and hummed. "Um, major giant. Dull blond hair. Big beard."

"Ohhh the brown bear, mhm." For a moment, Josie almost thought she saw June's lips twitch with a smile. "So what did he want?"

There was a pause of quiet as they turned right. "Yarn," June said, sounding as baffled by the word as Josie was. When Josie blinked at her, June shrugged. "He said he wanted to make a sweater."

"Huh. He did seem to like my macarons." There was that almost smile again. "Maybe he's like... a *Bear* bear. You know," Josie said as June frowned. "They're all living together. Maybe they're a gay biker gang."

June's fingers drummed on the steering wheel. "You hadn't considered it before?"

Josie shrugged, ignoring the stab of disappointment at the thought of Mr. Bad News being more interested in men than he might be in her. She did *not* need to have her eye on that man.

"I'm officially guilty of stereotyping," Josie said, smirking. "Probably in multiple directions since it took me until the knitting thing to consider it. Is it bad if I'm like... more charmed at the idea of all those scary dudes being gay?"

June huffed a brief laugh. "I have no idea, but I think you were right about them. I didn't smell brimstone but Ash... passed my wards as he came in, and it felt like a violation. Like someone had just broken into my house. I don't think he should've gotten in."

"Ash?"

June's lips pressed together as she turned left onto the road leading to the park. "That was his name."

Damn. Why hadn't Josie grabbed Mr. Bad News' name? *No. Bad Josie. Banish the man from your brain, girl.*

"I'll do a tarot reading later," June continued. "For now, Sheriff Nolan came in while he was there. Said tourists found evidence of some kind of ritual near the campsites. Including blood."

"Whoa! What? June, how did we take this car drive without you saying something before?" They passed Grimsby House, Josie's eyes straying out the car window to stare at the building. She knew the bikers were at the club, and the house was dark, but she rolled her eyes at herself for trying to find any evidence of them. It looked like the same old cute Victorian it had before they'd rolled into town. What was she expecting? Skull flags flying on the parapets? The house painted black? Fire in the windows?

"Nolan asked me to take a look at the spot. See if it looked like it was made by someone who knew what they were doing."

"Do you think it could be the bikers?" Josie asked.

The car rolled to a stop in front of the park sign. June turned off her lights, leaving the engine running in the dark for another moment. "Maybe. Or teenagers. I'm hoping teens, it is getting close to Halloween. But since you felt something when the men were in your shop yesterday, I was hoping maybe you could... pick up an energy?" She frowned at her own words.

"Okay, yeah. Let's hike."

The car stuttered into silence, and they stepped out and marched up the path. Josie was warm in the sweater June lent her—or gifted, depending on the washing situation—despite the bite of fall hanging in the air. The sky was rosy with sunset through the trees, and smoke traveled through the forest to the path, fragrant with meat cooking.

"Same tourists still camping?" Josie asked June. If the ones who'd found the ritual remnants were still around, they might be able to ask them questions, like if they'd heard anything in the night. Like a chicken squawking its last squawk.

"No. New ones. They should be out of the way."

They passed the campfire and tent from the opposite fork in the campsite paths, and Josie caught a glimpse of a young couple kissing by firelight, a marshmallow ignored and burning at the end of a skewer. Good. Those two definitely wouldn't notice her and June creeping around in the dark. On the other end of the campsites, Deputy Nolan— Sheriff Nolan's son—and a local ranger waited on a picnic table. The men tucked the beers in their hands behind them as they caught sight of the witches.

"Sorry for the wait," June said as they reached the park table where the men were waiting.

"Hey there," Mark Nolan greeted, jumping up from the table and pulling off his uniform hat, sweeping fingers through brown hair as he smiled at June. "No problem. Good to see ya!"

Poor guy, Josie thought. June's shoulders drew in and she nodded, her eyes searching the ground for the ritual marks.

"Hey Mark," Josie offered. She was no June Byrne, not to a guy like Mark who had probably been in love with June Byrne since elementary school, but at least Josie had manners when it came to saying hello. "So where's the spooky shit?"

June glared at her, and Josie stared back, willing her friend to be halfway human for once. They did not need the locals thinking that *they* were up in Merryweather doing blood rituals on the weekend. So it was time to play it cool.

"This way," the Ranger said, jerking his head behind him and away from the paths. He was a shorter guy, stocky, with a sunburn and the kind of unkempt beard on his chin that said he was either well into married life or determinedly single. "It's likely just kids," he said in a grunt.

Josie didn't blame him. If it weren't for the Sheriff knowing hints about their coven, he could've cleaned the site up and gone home hours ago, satisfied with his own assessment.

"That's what we figure," Josie said, letting a hint of her

old New Orleans drawl slide out. It'd been twenty years since Mama had dragged her north, and for the most part any accent was long gone by now. But Josie had learned over the years that there was something about sounding southern that made northerners smile and ease up, like they thought you were suddenly a redneck on their favorite TV show because you said 'y'all.'

Sure enough, the ranger relaxed, hooking his thumbs into his belt loop and letting his gut hang forward. *Men are simple, I swear*, Josie thought.

"Here it is," he said.

It took her a moment to spot the circle in the sweep of his arm. It was dark out, and a day of sitting out in the open left some of the marks softened in the earth and the blood long dried. What *did* catch Josie's eye was the knife. June stepped up to her side, gray eyes wide and fixed on the blade. It was simple, but not common. In fact, it was familiar and that was freaking them both out. Josie nudged June toward the knife, the *athame*—a ceremonial blade meant to direct energy, not *cut things*—now stained with crusted blood, and then took a slow walk around the circle.

"I'll see if I can make anything out of the marks," Josie said, crouching and squinting at the fading chalk in the grass. Squiggles mostly, nothing familiar. If it weren't for the athame, she would've said this was *absolutely* teenagers.

"If it'd just been spray paint and candles, I'd never've mentioned it to the Sheriff," the Ranger said.

Josie feigned balancing herself in her crouch, running her hand around the edge of the circle to see if there was any snap of magic. Nothing. Her gaze slid to June's and they stared at one another, trying to remain blank while feeling equally disturbed and confused.

"But with the blood, and that fancy looking knife..."

"I dunno about the blood, aside from they sell pig's at the butchers," Josie said, locking eyes with June as she continued, "But that knife looks like something a boy would probably order himself online."

June blinked, and then nodded. "Google makes it easier for amateurs to mimic real practitioners," she said.

One look at the two men, and Josie knew they thought "real" was a pretty subjective term when it came to this kind of thing. Which was better for their coven in the long run.

"The markings look like nonsense," Josie said, rising up. "Rinse it out and you should be good."

"What do you want to do with this?" June asked, pointing to the athame.

Nolan and the ranger looked at each other with dull, mulling confusion. "Throw it out, I s'pose," the ranger answered. "Don't look useful."

"You mind if I take it?" June asked.

Josie resisted the urge to turn and give her friend a massive *what the fuck* stare. They did not need these guys thinking there was anything of interest here! To the sheriff's department *or* to the coven.

But Mark Nolan was smitten. If June wanted a bloodied knife, then by god, that's what she'd get. "Don't see why not. S'not like it's a real crime scene or shit like that."

Josie cleared the laugh out of her throat before it could escape, and flashed June a look as she headed back toward the path.

"Just teenagers, fellas," Josie said.

"Wish my kid'd study for his homework the way some delinquents will for trouble making," the ranger muttered.

"Thanks for your help, June. Sure appreciate you coming up here. Imogen still up at the house alone?" he asked.

June stiffened and her steps leaned in Josie's direction, shying away from Mark. When she took too long to answer, Josie slid in.

"Sisters are more sisterly when they don't have to share a bathroom," she said, bumping shoulders with June.

Mark Nolan, who had a sister of his own, laughed loud and long, and stopped at the picnic table to finish his beer with the ranger.

"Have a nice evening ladies," the ranger offered, and Josie hustled to keep up with June as she motored down the hiking path back to her car.

Josie clicked her fingernails together as they walked, debating whether to say anything. June knew she knew where that knife came from, and it sure as hell wasn't a boy ordering online. That was Imogen's athame, and simple as it was, Josie knew there was no other like it because she'd heard June say their father had made them each one. June's was meant to look like a silver branch with a small blade at the end, but Imogen's was a long thin blade with a small handle, and it was currently crusted with blood and tucked into June's purse.

They reached the car and shut the doors behind them, and Josie couldn't keep her tongue still any longer. "I didn't feel any magic at the site."

"Neither did I," June whispered, staring blankly out the windshield.

Josie waited for her to start the car, but June only sat with her purse in her lap. "Definitely not Imogen's signature."

June's eyes flicked in Josie's direction. She looked... exhausted. Hollowed out. And a little like she was doubting whether or not she should've covered her sister's ass. If June was wondering if Imogen was involved with the ritual, how was Josie supposed to believe Imogen was innocent?

"I'll talk to her," June said. The keys missed the ignition twice before the car started, and June's head shook minutely on her shoulders. "In the morning. I need a drink."

Josie's eyes widened. "Alright. Let's hit up Gunney's."

6 GOOD TIMES AT GUNNEY'S TAVERN

Gunney's Tavern was only a slight improvement on the general atmosphere of Sweet Pea, in Bell's opinion. It was dimly lit, just a handful of bar lamps and the occasional illuminated beer logo hanging on the wall. There was a chalkboard menu behind the bar of pub food, with a printed out sign hanging above it that read 'If you want something that ain't microwaved go to High Top down the road.' The bartender was a middle aged woman with gray roots to her dark dye job, who yawned from her stool perch and had her nose buried in a romance novel.

But when the members of Hell's Bells stepped inside, the faces looking back at them weren't wearing expressions of fear or distrust, just the usual welcoming smile of the locals.

"What'll you have boys?" The bartender croaked without looking up.

Bell nodded Dante in her direction, and Aim and Barbie headed for the pool table, hovering behind two sunburnt men who still had sawdust on their work clothes. A fight would break out before the night was up, peace disrupted between the locals while the newcomers kept mostly to themselves in the shadows. Just a little light work for the evening.

Vinny stood behind Bell, scowling behind his red beard, and Bell narrowed his eyes at him. "Go find someone who looks like they're having as lousy a time as you are," Bell said, and Vinny snarled at him and paced to the back of the bar.

"I don't like his attitude," Bell said to Pie, watching Vinny's broad shoulders vanish and reappear under the bar lights.

"Part of his charm, according to HQ," Pie answered, eyes sliding sideways to Bell's, who wondered why the demon chose glasses to wear when he always seemed to look around their edges. "But he is a soldier on this mission. He may need to be reminded of that."

Bell grinned. "I invite you to tell him. For myself, I like waiting to see what kind of shit he thinks he can get away with around me."

Dante reappeared at Bell's side, sipping from a pint of dark ale. Bell raised an eyebrow and stared at the glass.

"Oh, I'm sorry," Dante purred in false surprise. "Did you want one?"

"You know perfectly well..." Bell started, but then the pretty demon's lion eyes were caught by a booth of women giggling in his direction, and he paced away before Bell could finish speaking.

"I'll get the booth," Ash said, a soft rumble from behind. "Grab me an IPA. Something hoppy."

The bartender held her finger up to Bell as he tried to order, her eyes wide on the pages of her book, thighs pressed together and cheeks flushed as she held her breath and read on.

"Gotta catch Chrissie before she gets to the smutty bits,"

an elderly man said to Bell out of the side of his mouth, and the line of patrons along the bar chuckled as Chrissie flipped him off and licked her lips as she read.

She was panting as she jumped down from her stool and put her hands on her hips, drawn-on eyebrow raising in indignation, as if Bell had caught her in the act itself instead of the reading of it. "Well? Watcha want?"

"Three lagers. Three IPAs," Bell said.

Someone at the end of the bar snorted, and Chrissie rolled her eyes and clenched her jaw, pointing to a hand-written list above her head. "We don't got those, and you gotta name the kind you want. I ain't here to help."

Given that was exactly what she was employed for, and she was unrepentantly rejecting her duty, Chrissie the bartender was Bell's favorite person in town he'd met yet. He grinned and leaned forward on the bar, propping his elbows on the ledge. The ire in her eyes melted slightly as she took him in, realizing the man in front of her was as much a fantasy as the one she'd been devouring off the page.

"Surprise me," Bell insisted.

Chrissie blushed, and the old man on Bell's left whistled low, eyes volleying between them as she smoothed down the wrinkle of her shorts, tugging at their fraying hem around her generous thighs, and pulling out some glasses from the stack.

"You a cheapskate?" she asked.

Bell pulled a fifty out of his pocket and set it on the counter. "Choose what ya like and keep the change," he said.

Chrissie preened, and the men at the bar laughed and returned to their conversations.

"You voting on the Merryweather Park sale next week?"

"Ehh, in my experience, County'll do as County pleases."

"Not sure I like the idea of Sweet Pea turning into a 'destination' like they're sayin'. Might go and vote against."

"Don't seem right to take a gift of land, and turn it out for a profit."

"A gift's a gift," Chrissie snapped to the greek chorus of Pabst drinkers as she sloshed Bell's pints over her fingers, knocking them down on the bar top. "It's up to the receiver to do as they please."

"We're talking about land, not jewelry, woman!" One man shouted back.

A bony elbow jostled against Bell's ribs, and he looked down at the old man who winked at him. "She fought harder to keep the ring than she did the fiancé."

"Oh piss on y'all!" Chrissie spat, and slammed the last beer down, half its contents jumping free of the glass, and the fifty dollar bill now thoroughly soaked.

Bell grabbed the glasses and dodged away from the conversation, finding Pie and Ashtaroth at a booth near the pool table. Aim and Barbie had started a team round of pool with the local friends, who were already growling at each other under their breath. Something about who could afford to lose the bet. Vinny and Dante were chatting up a table of young women, Dante's charms warming them up, as Vinny's snap and bite made them edgy and nervous.

Bell took a seat by Ash so he could watch the front of the bar, the beers he passed around the table leaving behind wet streaks.

"The boys are making headway," Ash said nodding toward the pool table. "Not so sure about the Casanovas."

"Dante could start a catfight if he felt like it," Bell said shrugging. "It's only our second night. Anyone know the significance of the Merryweather land?"

"The preserve up the road from the house?" Pie asked, taking a drink.

Bell nodded. "The County is considering selling it."

Pie's smile flickered above his striped beard, and Ash hummed. "Depending on whose hands that land ended up in..." Ash said, and Bell lifted his glass in a mild cheers.

"Could be a mess for little Sweet Pea," Bell said. "It's a starting point. There's a county meeting next week. Vote's in a month."

"Plenty of time," Pie said, relaxing back into the worn bench of the booth.

Movement at the front door caught Bell's eye, and he tensed in his seat as he watched the new arrivals walk in. The kitchen witch, petite and bouncing on the balls of her feet as she hurried to the bar before Chrissie got a chance to sit and take up her romance again. Behind her was a tall and willowy blonde, pale as a ghost with arms wrapped so tight around herself, she looked as if she was expecting to have an allergic reaction to the bar and its patrons.

"That's the stitch witch I mentioned," Ash said in Bell's ear, eyes equally fixed on the two women.

Bell grunted in answer, but his eyes strayed back to the other one. *Hello, Cupcake,* he thought, perhaps too enthusiastically because she stiffened at the bar, and her head whipped over her shoulder, gaze immediately finding him. He grinned as she glared, and his fingers itched to reach through the air and guide her steps to him, see if she still smelled like vanilla and cinnamon outside of her little pink shop. Without the apron, he could see the curves of her, wrapped in soft halo pink and skintight black jeans. She turned to the other witch and rose up to her toes to whisper in her ear, no doubt warning her friend of their presence.

What had she decided about them? Bell doubted a

human, even a witch, would believe there were demons walking on earth, tasked with disrupting the peace of a sleepy little hill town. It made him want to flash fire in his stare at her, grin with a wolf's mouth, reveal himself and see if she ran, or if she just kept giving him that 'don't fucking start' look.

The stitch witch took one look at them and turned back to the door, but Josie wrapped a small hand around her sleeve and held her still, whispering rapidly in her ear. Ash was as tense as Bell was, and Bell tore his attention away from the women to tilt his head in his soldier's direction.

"You think you can break that one?"

There was a whiff of heavy gasoline on the air, and then it vanished and Ash relaxed backwards against the corner of the booth. "I think I can get through the wall she has up. No telling what then," he said with a shrug.

A moment later, Josie the kitchen witch was dragging her friend in their direction, the tall glasses in their hands glittering with something stronger than beer, if Bell had to guess. He had barely scooted in, shoulder to shoulder with Ashtaroth's enormous frame, before Josie was throwing herself down in the seat next to him, all but tossing the stitch witch down next to Pie.

"Cupcake," Bell said.

"Mr. Bad News," she said, and then scowled at him as his grin widened.

Ash chuckled. "Not a bad name for you, Bell. Hello again, June."

June, the stitch witch, only blinked at him, her lips pressed tight together, refusing to join the name game.

"Bell," he said, pointing to himself and then around the table. "Ash. Pie. How can we help you ladies?"

"What are you doing in Sweet Pea?" Josie asked, eyes

narrowing at him, a flush high in her cheeks turning tawny brown to a flattering shade of rose. Bell opened his mouth to answer, but she cut him off, words rapid fire like a machine gun running the demons down. "And what the hell are seven grown ass men doing moving into a house together like a bunch of frat boys? And why do you smell weird?"

"Josie," June breathed, eyes wide and silver in awe or horror.

"Construction work," Pie answered. "Paint fumes."

"It's *not* paint fumes," Josie said, rolling her eyes at him. "Pie like the pastry or Pi like the math?"

"What kind of engine you got up there?" Bell asked, reaching up and tapping on Josie's forehead, before promptly having his hand knocked away. She felt as soft as that sweater looked. "You run faster than my bike."

"You fuckers are *wrong* somehow, and I wanna know why," Josie growled at him.

Bell wanted to pick her up by her tiny waist, set her down on the table in front of him, and let her fire pestering, nosy, rude questions at him all day for his amusement. Instead, he lifted his hand up, showing three fingers.

"One. We heard it was a nice place with nice people," he said, pulling down his index finger and then 'tsk'ing her for proving that statement wrong. "Two, saving money." He tucked his ring finger down and raised his eyebrows, saying slowly, "Three. Fuck you."

Josie stared at his middle finger for two whole seconds, before a grin slanted across her lips and she huffed, turning to face a frozen June. She lifted her glass, chewing on the end of her straw. "Bullshit," she said, shoulders dropping.

"You don't see many motorcyclists here in Sweet Pea?" Pie asked.

"Of course we do, but you're..." June trailed off, her wide

eyes caught on Ash for a moment too long, before dropping to her drink.

"You're a motorcycle *crew*. Not just a bunch of retired beer bellies touring the country," Josie finished for her, eyes studying them, long black lashes nearly covering her stare. "And I don't believe for a minute you're here 'cause you like the scenery."

Bell leaned toward her, and her spine straightened, iron strong. "I'm acquiring a taste for it," he said, drinking her in.

If Ash wanted to break the skittish stitch witch, then perhaps Bell should set his sights on this one. Not breaking. *Defeating*. And to set that trap, he might need to lay bait. Which shouldn't be too hard. Those feather lashes blinked, and he caught her pupils dilating as he smiled at her, adding a little shine just for good measure.

"Man, I fucking *told* you!"

"Shit, you did not!"

Josie twisted at the end of the bench, and Bell sat up, looking over the back of the booth to watch the two friends who'd been playing pool against his men break out into shoving hands on chests and snarling in each other's faces. Aim and Barbie strolled slowly away from the scene, in the direction of their booth, shoulders rolling with the victory of small chaos.

"Come on, Junebug," Josie said, sliding out of the seat before Bell could catch her. She snared her friend by the elbow and nodded at a frowning Barbie. "Seats are yours, boys."

"We keepin' company with witches, Bell?" Aim asked, and Bell swallowed the growl in his throat as Aim admired Josie's swinging hips as she walked away.

"We do if it serves the cause," Bell said. "For now, we

better get back to the club. I wanna be open for business before next week."

They downed their beers in one go and rose from the booth. Dante's eyebrows twitched in interest, his expression bored despite the three young women doing their absolute best to keep his attention. Vinny had the fourth girl cornered, his beard on her throat as her lips hung open, chest panting and eyes fixed as wide as full moons up on the ceiling.

"Back to work, if you don't mind," Bell called to them.

Dante untangled himself from the girls, but Vinny took his sweet time, lifting his hand from under the counter and sucking on his fingers. The girl he'd been treating, or tormenting, whimpered and sagged against the wall, her face equal parts disappointed and relieved.

"S'dull as doornails round here," Vinny muttered, leaping out of the booth over the back of the seat.

Whispers followed the crew's backs as they headed to the door, and Bell stared too long at Josie's back, waiting for her to turn at the bar and give him a parting look, preferably an irritated one. Her cheek twitched in his direction and then she turned to June, eyes out of his sight.

7

The Fall Colors

There was a trail of ash and sulfur poisoning the air down the hill from the front of Imogen's cabin, onto Merryweather Preserve. Imogen took slow steps, catching flickers of heat on her fingertips as she followed the darkness, whisper soft brushes of razor edged power stinging her cheeks. This was what Josie spoke of at the coven meeting, and Imogen wondered if any of the others really understood what it meant. When you only worked in light magic, you forgot to prepare yourself for the darkest shades. Imogen Byrne was well versed in shadows.

The wards Imogen set around Sweet Pea had run sirens through her bones every hour for the past two days, warning her of an invasion across the border she'd built, dangerous and potent. One wearing the forms of men, apparently.

Imogen parted her lips and closed her eyes, lifting her face to the slow rise of the sun up the hill, and let the air she breathed in draw a flavor on her tongue. She coughed at the scourging sting, and tears rose to her eyes, all the moisture in her throat drying up as if she'd just stepped into an oven.

Demons. In little Sweet Pea.

She opened her eyes, a headache already picking a slow and steady beat in her skull, calling her back to bed, to the dark of the cabin. Except that the stench was only across the road from the cabin, and Imogen wanted to know how far the trail went. Had they started outside her window, or found their way to it?

If the beasts were in town because of *her*, then she had heavy lifting to do and soon, before one of them got their hooks into anyone else in the town.

Like June, she thought.

Not June though. June was impervious. June was a cage made of diamond. She would be safe, even from demons. Even from Imogen.

Imogen opened her eyes and winced at the light, the glitter of gold and fire creeping up from the roots of the trees. When was the last time she'd left the cabin when the sun was up?

She caught the blade's scratch of power on her cheek, strangely gentle and dangerous at the same time, and followed it down the hill, closer to the hiking paths. The trail crossed over a path and back into the wild, wandering aimlessly, layering over the territories where Imogen had worked magic. It was possible she was following a trail that only chased her own. Perhaps she was being hunted.

The drowsy exhaustion and queasy discomfort sharpened inside of Imogen. If the demons had stopped to see Josie first, did that mean the entire coven was at risk? Her hands shook at her side, and her veins felt hollow and cold, bloodless under pale skin, craving power or something to dull the hunger. The demon's trail led to the main path out of the preserve and onto the road leading to Grimsby House. Imogen considered walking there now, but her tools were hidden somewhere in the trees, and she hadn't closed her eyes and slept since the night before.

Imogen turned back to the preserve and listened to the quiet, the waking birdsong, the breeze drawing down the fall colors tourists came to see—ruby and bitter yellow and every shade of orange. It was time to get her tools out of their hiding place. The sun, still dim in the early hour, already felt like a scorching brand on the back of her neck, and she pulled her hair down to guard her skin as she walked.

She made it nearly to the campsite, halfway to the hollow tree where she hid her ritual tools the last time she worked out here alone, when the whiff of demon was gone and something worse had replaced it in the air. Tangy and sharp and rich, it burned inside Imogen's nose, and her stomach coiled like a snake in response.

Turn back. Take a black bath and sleep in the visions. Back to the cabin.

The whispers or warnings sounded too close to the ancient voice that haunted her, and Imogen followed the path until she saw it.

A bloodied hand, reaching out onto the foot-beaten gravel, the young man's body barely covered by a night's fall of leaves, ruby maple mixing with bitter blood brown. A breeze picked a leaf off a pale blue cheek, revealing an open eye, his mouth and neck painted with gore and still sticky. A small black bug crawled across his jaw, and Imogen didn't know which was worse, breathing through her nose or her mouth, so she stopped breathing altogether.

Sunlight hit the forest green tent on the campsite, door unzipped and another body hanging facedown out of the opening, her hair ebony black and matted with blood.

The Lich. The Lich is back, Imogen thought, heart racing

and breath trapped in her chest. *Daddy bent to the left on the basement stairs, his neck crooked. Mom suspended from the slow turning ceiling fan.*

Imogen blinked, replacing the horrors of memory with the current disaster.

The Lich was gone, but there *were* demons.

Imogen turned away from the scene, eyes squeezing shut on the sun burning through branches, and swallowed the bile rising up her throat. She would walk home, like she should have before, and fill the tub with charcoal and scalding hot water. She would wait for June to call with the news.

Murder in Sweet Pea.

My fault as usual.

THE LOWER BASEMENT was the quietest place in the cabin. Once the Byrne family wine cellar—its contents now drained—Imogen found it the perfect place to work. Dark and quiet, stripped of shelves until there was nothing but dark polished brick. She lay stretched out on her back, hands open and up at her sides, head turned to the left to watch the candle.

The flame in front of her was hungry for air in the dry room, its swishing cat's tail tip rising as tall as Imogen's head. The bricks shifted and turned and crawled on the walls around her, shadows waiting to melt down to the floor and speak to her call. The candle flame flashed wide, crow's wings beating together and then blending to a horse's head tossing, mane flipping.

Imogen.

There. The shadows were coming.

"Imogen!"

Shit, Imogen thought.

"Imogen, are you home?"

The flame was a knife, small handle and long blade familiar, and then the door to the cellar cracked open and light bled into the room from the hall, shadows retreating and flame sinking into the mild mannered fingertip of any other candle.

"Imogen!"

June rushed in, her knees crashing at her sister's side, her rush blowing the candle out with a little spit and a puff of smoke. June's hands were on Imogen's face, too firm to pull away, and Imogen released a small whimper. The touch felt like pegs hammering into her bones, pinning her to the floor. June pried Imogen's eyes wide, and through the curtain of blonde hair Imogen missed June's expression. Which was good. It was a too familiar one.

"Oh, Gin." Already, the worry in June's voice was receding, settling into a hard acceptance.

"Sleeping pills. And mushrooms," Imogen said, before June had to ask. It was better when they didn't play that game.

"Where are you getting them?"

The pills. June knew the mushrooms were growing in the basement over their heads, and no number of arguments or destroying Imogen's wares had done any good.

"Dr. Holloway," Imogen said.

With her face shadowed and her hair pale as bone, June could've been the Lich disguising itself as Imogen's sister. But no dark spirit could imitate June's resigned disappointment so perfectly. She sighed, sinking back to sit on her heels, and finally the light caught her face. Imogen's lips curled as she gazed up at her sister. June was good, she *shone*.

"What's wrong?" Imogen asked, finding June's hand on her thigh. Her fingers felt like gold, strong and malleable and warm, gripping tight to Imogen's.

June's eyes blinked, watering one moment and clear the next, and the answer was unspoken between them. Imogen was the thing wrong in June's life.

"There's been a murder. At Merryweather," June said, sweeping her hair back from her face, strands moving like water through her fingers. Imogen reached up to feel if they were wet, and June frowned and caught the hand before she could touch.

"I know. I found them."

"You *what*?" June took in a deep breath, and Imogen shut her eyes when the walls breathed with her sister. The psychedelics in the mushrooms helped make scrying and trance work vivid and expansive. They didn't help when family arrived and wanted to have a serious conversation.

"I went for a walk this morning," Imogen said. "I saw the bodies."

"You were the one that called them in?"

Imogen shook her head, and June's breath hitched. "I saw them. And then I came back home."

With the door to the hall open, whispers of the world were crawling into the room, and Imogen couldn't separate what might have been left from the scrying link, and what were ambient sounds of the house. Strong fingers clamped around her arms, and she winced at the iron grip as June dragged her up to her feet.

"Are you... Imogen! Why?" June's voice was breaking, breaths too loud in Imogen's ears, and she stumbled back,

June's grip following her and then dragging her out into the hall and up the stairs.

"I was tired," Imogen whispered.

"And if- if they find some kind of evidence that you were there? Then what?"

"Then I'll tell them I saw the bodies and went home. Or I'll fix it."

June shook Imogen at the top of the stairs, until Imogen's eyes were open. The house was too bright, and June had yanked the shades back from the windows and made it worse.

"Don't joke! If you aren't joking, then don't *say* things like that! You promised me, Gin. You *promised*."

"I promised," Imogen repeated, nodding, trying not to see the shades of red in the room—the pillows on the couch, her coat hanging on the peg—as the color dripped like blood in her vision. "No magic."

"No manipulative magic. No dark magic. No spirits. Don't think I don't know what you were doing in the cellar. That's not the kind of scrying we agreed on."

"No murder," Imogen said. "No *more* murder."

June's hands were off her. Imogen's eyes closed again, and she was floating in nothing and somehow surrounded, buried, suffocating. "I can't deal with you while you're like this."

June's footsteps were drumbeats as she paced the floor, and Imogen groaned and covered her face with her hands as the headache from this morning returned with a vengeance. Something rustled, nails scratching up her back, and then warm fingers stroked the back of her wrists, gentle and careful. Imogen pulled her hands down again, eyes squinting to keep out the light. Between them, June held Imogen's athame.

Imogen tried to snatch it, to rescue it from her sister's grip. June knew better. She shouldn't touch it!

"Don't," June said. "The Ranger's and Sheriff's department found this at another ritual site yesterday. It had blood on it. And they let me take it, because they thought it was just kids goofing off."

"What kind of ritual site?"

"A fake one, as far as I could tell. Not yours. But how did it get there, Gin?"

"I had it stashed in a hollow tree."

"Your *athame*?" Imogen reached for it again, and June pulled it out of her reach. "I'm sorry. I know, but you can't have this back right now. I have to take it to the Sheriff's department. I had to put it through the dishwasher because I knew what they would find. *Your* fingerprints, Gin. Which they have in the system because..."

Because Imogen had killed their parents.

The sisters stood in still silence, red color dripping at the corners of Imogen's vision like a leaky faucet. June was brightness itself in front of her, and Imogen shut her eyes as June stepped forward. June's hands were empty as her fingertips brushed across the tops of Imogen's cheeks, streaking wetness on her skin. Blood?

"I'm sorry," June whispered, her voice tight.

Tears. Imogen's tears.

"Are you tired?"

Imogen nodded, and arms curled around her. She leaned into June as she shuffled them both through the house and up to the loft. It was dark up there, and Imogen sighed and softened as June laid her down in bed. June sat, her hip against Imogen, and brushed strands of hair off her face like their mother had when they were little girls.

"I didn't kill them."

"I know you didn't, Gin. It was an accident."

"No, June. The campers. I didn't kill them." The death of their parents could never be called an accident.

June's touch stilled, and then she bent, pressing a kiss to Imogen's forehead, warmth seeping into her skin. "Never even crossed my mind, Gin."

Lie, a voice whispered in Imogen's thoughts or from the corner of the room.

"Time to rest," June said. "We'll figure this all out. Promise."

8 LOVE THY NEIGHBOR

Rosa lived in a converted carriage house up on Tillyman Road, just a couple houses down from old Grimsby House. The owners of the property and the front house were a pair of elderly men, who had offered Rosa the space after she'd given them a generous deal on their wedding flowers. Thurman and Cornell allowed Rosa use of their wrap-around porch whenever she pleased. When she and Josie parked themselves on the loveseat with a bottle of wine between them, the couple would open the window by their Victrola and play old jazz records. The same ones Josie's Mémé would play after Sunday dinners; Fats Domino, Ella and Louis, Sarah Vaughn, and Jelly Roll Morton.

It was too chilly in Sweet Pea's high altitude October to really feel like New Orleans any time of the year, but Josie always felt the mood Cornell and Thurman offered was close enough.

The night after the murder, even with the bottle of red between them, there was no music on the Victrola. Instead, Thurman and Cornell stood out on their porch steps with

Josie and Rosa, and the four of them stared at the flashing lights at the end of the street.

"Just a sweet young couple up here on their fall break," Thurman said, 'tsk'ing his tongue against the back of his teeth and shaking his head.

"Oh don't, Thu. It's too much," Cornell said, sighing and peering through his round glasses with a keen stare. His elbow nudged at Josie's, and she poured another inch of cabernet into his glass.

Up the road, coming from town, the roar of engines grew dense and powerful.

"What do you think of your new neighbors?" Josie asked, her eyes turning away from the emergency lights, waiting to see the first glimpse of the motorcycles.

"Oh those boys?" Cornell said, cat's smile stretching across his lips—stained a deep berry color with the wine on his brown skin. "I'm sure they're quite sweet." Rosa and Josie exchanged a brief, skeptical look as Cornell continued to nod. "One of them helped me carry out the trash this morning. Big, tight muscles on his arms. I used to have muscles like that, didn't I, Thu?"

Over Cornell's diminutive height, Thurman shook his head at Josie, salt and pepper hair curling around his ears. Thurman reminded Josie of what Mr. Rogers might look like if he'd smoked a lot of weed.

"We used to ride motorcycles, back in the day," Cornell said.

"Still have the bikes in the garage," Thurman said. "I've half a mind to take mine out for a spin to their new club, just for a laugh. Heard they're looking for new members."

"You should join," Josie said, grinning at the men. She'd like to see Bell's expression as they walked in to his super macho and manly club too.

The headlights were appearing, fine pinpoints at the end of the street, spread out across both narrow lanes.

"Wouldn't that be fun?" Cornell said, perking up. "If they'd have us."

"Don't take no for an answer," Rosa said, shrugging. "We know you know how, Cornie."

Cornell shrugged as the others tried to contain their laughs. As a prosecutor for the district attorney, Cornell Green could find himself a legal door into that motorcycle club, if not open it himself with his own personal persistence and talent for argument.

"You don't think one of them had something to do with… you know?" Rosa asked, nodding her head toward Merryweather Preserve.

Cornell eyed Rosa over his tortoise-shell glasses. "I should think we know better than to judge based on appearances, don't we Rosie-love?"

"Oh hush, we all know it's the appearances you like so much on those boys," Thurman said.

The bikers pulled onto their pretty brick drive, but all their heads were turned to face the red and blue glow at the end of the street. As soon as they were parked, those black boots were headed in their direction. Josie's eyes were glued to Bell, Mr. Bad News. She thought her own name for him suited him better. If he was a bell, it was one of those great ominous things on top of a crumbling cathedral, and even that wasn't right.

No. Bell was black coffee with dark whiskey, and a bit of careless cigarette ash floating on the surface. Basically, he was what Josie should absolutely not want to drink down in one gulp.

"Lost hiker?" he asked as he and his men arrived in front of the Greens' front porch.

"Double homicide," Cornell said, eyes on the woods.

But Josie was watching Beleth. He looked surprised, eyebrows ticking up for a beat. And *then* he turned his head to look at his men. Rosa's fingers pried Josie's grip off her wrist, but Josie refused to stop staring at the men, watching the minute shift of expressions on the bikers' faces. She had a very clear impression that Bell was asking his men if they knew anything about the murder, without speaking a word, and she didn't think he was asking if they'd *heard* the news. Their answers were less clear. Ash and Pie were watching the officials down the road. The mismatched pair shrugged in unison at Bell, and the other two—the movie star and the mean looking redhead—just blinked in response.

"Where were you guys last night, by the way?" Josie asked.

Thurman and Cornell choked on their wine, and Rosa let out a great cackle of laughter, head thrown back.

"Now, now, Miss Benoit," Cornell cooed, his eyebrows raised and a rich southern accent drawling out. "Let's not be inhospitable to the newcomers. You boys like a beer while we rubberneck?"

"Beer'd be great," Mean mug said, a false grin flashing through the manicured beard, flame orange licking down the sides of his jaw.

"Come on, Thu, let's leave the ladies to interrogate the young men while we hunt down some bottles," Cornell said.

The bikers watched Cornell and Thurman head back inside, and Josie tensed, squaring herself at the top of the step as if she alone could protect the house. Rosa leaned up against the pillar and watched the scene like it was sport. So much for moral support amongst the coven.

"You gotta be careful who you go around accusin' of murder, Cupcake," Bell said, hand reaching out and cupping

Mean Mug's shoulder before the snarling redhead could step closer. "Vinny never developed a sense of humor."

"Vinny suits you," Josie said to the redhead. Vinny was a name that sounded like someone you called when you needed a 'situation' cleaned up. Although this Vinny looked more like he enjoyed making messes. Josie let her gaze travel over the ruggedly handsome faces of the others. "Rosa, that there is Pie, and Ash. And Mr. Bad News says his name is Bell."

"Cheers," Rosa murmured, her brown eyes sizing up Pie, who seemed oblivious.

"What's the rest of the roster?" Josie asked, looking at the other three.

Bell introduced them. Dante was an alright sort of regular name, and it looked good on Movie Star, although there probably wasn't much that looked bad on him. Aim, the towering and smiling black man, was a name that made her wonder what he was aiming and where—a possible cause for concern. The last one though...

"Barbie," she sounded out slowly, eyebrows raising. "Are you a...fan of hers?"

Barbie was the unwashed one with a constantly furrowed brow and tattoos up to his chin, and Josie didn't think he'd chosen the name for irony because he just... didn't seem to get it.

"Who?" he asked in a soft grunt, looking to Aim.

"Oh my," Rosa whispered, eyes huge, and lips pursed tight to hold in her laugh.

What was stranger than the fact that Barbie didn't seem to know his own namesake, was that none of the other men seemed to find it funny either.

"We were home last night," Bell said, drawing Josie's attention back. His smile was a hard edged line on his face, but there was laughter in his eyes. She just couldn't tell if it was at her expense or not. "I'm sure our neighbors noted our arrival."

It would be hard to miss the sound of seven motorcycles in this quiet neighborhood, but it didn't mean one of the men couldn't sneak out to the woods on foot.

"Not a super solid alibi," Josie said, trying to sort out what she found so thrilling about the way Bell's grin grew at her answer.

"Hey," Rosa said, straightening up off the pillar to nudge her hip against Josie's, and pointing to the sidewalk across the street.

Josie followed the pointed finger and frowned. Imogen Byrne was standing in an oversized sweater on the other side of the street, staring at the pack of men between them. Rosa grabbed onto Josie's arm and dragged her down the stairs, directly through the crowd of men, her round nose wiggling and eyebrows raising at Josie as if to say 'oh yeah, brimstone.' Or at least that's what Josie assumed the face meant, because she definitely caught those whiffs of smoke again while cutting by Vinny.

"Hey, Imogen!" Rosa called. She brushed up against Pie, smiling and batting thick lashes in his face. "Excuse me, honey."

The bikers turned to watch them as they crossed the street, and Josie was just passing Dante—the extra handsome one— when his own stare found Imogen and he stiffened, eyes flashing strangely as if the red light of the police cars had bounced off them, the color matching the warm glint off a copper penny. Even stranger, Imogen's was fixed on him too. Josie might have thought it was an epic case of eye-fucking, except that Imogen didn't look aroused, she looked...dangerous.

"Dantalion," Imogen said, stepping down from the sidewalk. Josie and Rosa fell in beside her, and Josie thought Imogen seemed to grow in size as she moved closer, putting herself in front of her friends. Imogen's sweater brushed against the back of Josie's hand, biting with the static electric gathering of magic.

"Basement witch," Dante answered her, his tan hands sliding into jean pockets as his eyes raked over Imogen.

"What kind of name is Dantalion?" Rosa murmured in Josie's ear.

"Basement witch?" Vinny asked Dante.

This feels like a scene out of a western...or a dance battle movie, Josie thought, and then Imogen turned and looked her in the eye.

"Dantalion is a demon's name," Imogen said.

Vinny hissed, and the other men tensed. *Brimstone,* Josie thought. *Of course.* Bell was at the back of the crowd of men, the crowd of *demons,* with his arms crossed and a lazy, insincere smile on his mouth. Whatever Cornell and Thurman were up to, Josie was glad they were still in the house for this conversation.

"How do you know they're demons?" Josie asked Imogen.

"Because she summoned me," Dante said. He grinned at Imogen, and that strange metallic orange flashed in his stare again. "Surprised I didn't hear from you again, witch."

"You served your purpose," Imogen said in her soft, simple, withdrawn way. Then she looked down and turned to Josie again. "This was before the coven," she whispered, almost as if in apology.

Josie suddenly wanted a timeout in the conversation. Shit. Imogen's athame in the woods and the blood... would Josie really be able to say for certain she knew what symbols were needed to call demons? She doubted very much June would have said anything to her if Josie hadn't recognized the athame as Imogen's. This whole night was messy, and Josie wished she knew how to banish demons and maybe Imogen too, just in case.

"Well, alright. Seven demons," Rosa said, but her skin was paler than usual, freckles standing out stark on her cheeks. Josie found her hand between them and squeezed it tight.

"And three witches," Vinny answered with a sneer.

"Four," Pie corrected. "The stitch witch isn't here."

In that moment, Josie would've bet on delicate Imogen in any fight. The woman was in front of Pie in two quick strides, her hands loose at her sides but tension running through every line of her body, even the long strawberry blonde hair running down her back.

"If I see a single one of you take a step toward my sister, I will have you bound up, inside out, in a place so dark you'll dream of Hell like it's Disneyland as you stare at your own navel for eternity."

Rosa vibrated with fear or excitement, and Josie swore she'd lost her breath entirely. Who the fuck was *this* Imogen, and where had she been on Saturday nights at Gunney's? To his credit, Pie the demon only nodded, slow and shallow. He didn't look spooked, but he wasn't growling under his breath like Vinny, who was now trapped behind the shoulders of Ash and Bell while they waited patiently for Imogen to step back.

"We aren't here to murder the tourists. Your coven doesn't need to concern itself with us," Bell said in that soft purring tone of his. Josie found herself locking gazes with him, and she wondered how he'd respond if it was him Imogen threatened. She thought he might only laugh.

"Your time here is limited," Imogen answered him. She relaxed and turned her back on the men. Josie saw dark, exhausted circles under her eyes, when only a second ago Imogen had been electrified. Now she was slumping, fingers trembling slightly as she tucked them under crossed arms. "Go inside Rosa's where it's warded," Imogen said. Without another glance, she passed them and took the sidewalk to the end of the block, walking home up the hill.

"What're y'all doin out in the street? Beer's up here," Cornell called, his hands full of bottles as he walked back onto the porch.

One by one, the demons turned heel in their boots, strolling up to the palatial front porch and parking themselves on steps and railings.

"What do we do?" Josie whispered to Rosa. Her own mind was reeling. Demons. Demons from...Hell?

How many other places are they coming from, Josie?

"I'm not locking myself inside and leaving Cornie and Thu with a pack of demons, even if there are police down the street," Rosa said, worried gaze falling on her landlords.

"Well yeah, but, *demons*. Here? And did you miss the part where Imogen was *summoning* them?"

"Past tense," Rosa said at a rapid pace. "But no, I didn't miss that. And after that speech, I think I'm a little too scared to ask her why. Come on. Tonight we guard our old men. Tomorrow we tackle...this whole damn mess, I guess."

Josie looked at the emergency vehicles at the entrance to Merryweather, and then to the denim and leather clad demons who sprawled around the beautiful old porch she'd always felt so at home on. 'This damn mess' was starting to look a little too big to tackle in one go.

But she would sure as shit be willing to get a head start on it.

9 THE APPETITE OF DEMONS

Dantalion was not the kind of demon Bell would have chosen for his mission. The former angel had fallen, not out of support with his brethren, but in self-interest. But the Great Duke of Hell had gained a reputation in the Bowels for his finesse on the ground, if not his work ethic. For instance, Bell was pretty sure Dante hadn't actually lifted a single finger to help clean up their club house, but he always *looked* busy.

"You wanna tell me what the witch from last night summoned you for?" Bell asked, rolling out the strain in his shoulders from nailing up sheets of chrome to the stripped walls of the club. The secret he'd sniffed out their first night came to an early head when they'd confronted the witches. Of course, another secret had come out too; the witches knew what they were, and Bell felt that was a comparative loss in the scheme of the battle.

"Something to do with her sister," Dante said, shrugging and pushing around a table that had already been pushed from one end of the room and back.

"The stitch witch?" Ash asked. He stood next to Bell,

holding sheet metal in place to be nailed to the wall, and he perked up at the mention of the witch he'd asked permission to toy with.

Bell had granted the permission, but was wondering if that was a mistake. The whole situation was starting to look at little too intertwined, and the threat Imogen delivered to them last night hadn't sounded idle. If she was the one casting dark magic in the woods, and apparently summoning his men in the past, she might have the skill to throw them into some dark dimension.

Dante shrugged again, spinning a chair around and sitting backwards in the seat. "Guess so. I didn't get a lot of details. Just... laid back and served my purpose." His eyebrows waggled slightly, and a satisfied smile curled the corners of his lips.

Sex magic? Witches had called on their kind for the like plenty in the past. A quick romp in a sacred circle could boost powers for necessary workings, provided the witch was careful not to smudge the salt or chalk that kept the demon bound. Even Beleth had been known to partake. There were worse ways to serve when summoned, but it wasn't the kind of magic he would've guessed the sugary sweet coven to be working. Which made this pale witch an interesting anomaly, or a dangerous one.

"I do know one thing though. She needed the magic to bind her sister."

Ash's eyes narrowed. "June's got plenty of power."

"Not her magic," Dante said, eyes glinting copper. "Emotions."

Ash blinked and glanced at Beleth. So that was what had the stitch witch so bottled up.

"Can you unbind her?" Beleth asked. That might make for a curious influence.

"Not without direct orders from the caster," Dante said. He pushed himself back out of the chair, stretching.

Ash grunted and frowned. "Could make my work difficult," he said.

"Maybe. Maybe not. You and Dante find out what the binding is about. Maybe unwrapping the stitch witch is exactly the kind of project you need," Bell said, rearranging the battle pieces in his head.

Ash nodded and left to follow and quiz Dante, and Bell put down the nail gun, stepping back from his work. The club was coming along. The burgundy was gone, and Ash had done some kind of bar top glass mosaic with the lamps Bell let Barbie shatter. The pool table was gone, and the old chairs were out, replaced with painted, black, wooden seats that Ashtaroth had set his mind to. Low-wattage bulbs hung without covers, turning the room slightly orangey. As a space it was underdone, but more than that and it would've started blending in with the town's love of excessive decor.

"It's an improvement," he said to Pie, who'd just finished laying the refurbished wood flooring.

"The club needs members," Pie said, watching the door.

As if Bell's fellow King had conjured the sight, out on the street a motorbike came stuttering into view, its rider jerking the machine into a parking spot in front of the club. Off the seat rose Danny Lin—just out of high school and working at the hardware store. The kid was shy and appeared to be terrified of every single member of the Hell's Bells MC. But he had shown up, which was more than Bell could say of anyone they tried to recruit out of Gunney's.

"Give him something useful to do," Bell said. "I'm going to grab some food."

"We need to figure out what we're doing with this space," Pie said.

"After I get back."

Pie nodded and headed for the front door where Danny was taking an extraordinary amount of time to work up the nerve to come inside. Bell slid out the back, letting the door click shut behind him. For once, the sun was not shining in Sweet Pea. He stretched in the empty alley, his bones making satisfying and unnatural cracking sounds, wanting to burst free of the skin he'd invented for himself. The snap and creak of joints was followed by a growl of hunger in his gut, and Bell grimaced.

Human forms were so needy.

His stomach growled again, and he did a last twist to work the kinks out in his spine. He'd cut up the alley, see what smelled good on Main Street, and avoid the worst of the friendly local traffic. Except everything smelled like grease, or the burning of espresso beans behind the cafe. The best thing about being out of the Bowels again was having taste buds, and he didn't want to waste them on trash. He almost gave up the search—he may have a hungry human form, but he was a demon and there was no starving to death in his future—when sweet pastry and spice and vanilla floated over the roofs of the shops.

There was an animal sound from his gut. He might be willing to starve, but his stomach was not and it had just made up its mind. Bell ducked out of the alley and turned the corner back onto Main. Josephine's was just two doors down, and from this side of the street none of his men would see him slipping inside.

They'll smell the sugar when I show up again. But so what? He was the leader of this mission. If he wanted to corrupt a witch for a bit of fun on the side, that's what he'd fucking do. He steadfastly ignored the risks he'd considered just minutes before.

The bells on the front door were sweeter as he walked in this time, music preceding his arrival. That didn't stop the woman behind the counter from going stiff with awareness, her back facing him. A blush of color rose up out of the collar of her black t-shirt, right into the close shave of her hair on her head.

The shop was busy. It was Saturday, and there were young girls crowded around one table, two older couples at the others, and a few people in line at her counter. The flavor of the air was wistful, full of daydreams and fond memories and the delicate joy of cheating on a diet. Bell popped the daydreams like iridescent bubbles floating in front of his face, and then frowned as they popped right back up again.

Pre-teens were irritatingly optimistic.

He watched as Josie forced smiles for her customers, tension in every movement, frustration flickering behind her eyes as the man at the front of the counter—dressed in a business suit on a Saturday like an asshole—debated on what to order. Her left shoulder bobbed slightly as she waited, her heel popping against the floor with impatience.

"You don't have a gluten-free option for the croissant?"

"Just the scones, cookies, and muffins," Josie bit out, and when the businessman's stare turned to her she flipped on that tight smile that didn't reach her eyes. The man turned back to the case, 'hmph'ing, and the smile vanished just as quick.

Bell bore a stare into the back of the man's head, digging for information.

Chad Schmidt, property developer, did not have food allergies, but he thought he could probably put a shop like Josephine's Bakery out of business if he grabbed the land rights to Merryweather in the inevitable sale. He'd make a ritzy complex of shops and rental homes inside of the scenic site, redirect the money flow of tourism there instead of on quaint little Sweet Pea's Main Street, and the local businesses would get crushed beneath. Exactly the kind of player in the long game that Bell needed.

"Three croissants and a gluten-free blueberry scone."

Josie was quick to bag the order, as if she already knew what the man would say. Bell watched the man head for the door, raising the paper bag up to his nose and taking a whiff. Schmidt was a man in his late forties trying to look in his early thirties, with dyed blond hair and a fading tan. One sniff of pastry and something was softening in his expression, that bubble of contentment building inside of him. Bell squashed it out and stepped forward in line.

When she had served her local customers with the efficiency of predictable orders, and the cluster of young girls had left their table empty and full of dishes, Bell reached the front of the line. Josie didn't bother with a smile, he covered her sight of the rest of the shop and no one could see her openly glaring up at him from behind his broad shoulders.

"What do you want?" she said, quiet enough for privacy.

"Food." She raised one eyebrow. Her question remained. "Surprise me again," he said.

And then, in a somewhat embarrassing moment for him, his stomach growled loud enough for the whole shop to hear, echoing off the tile. Her lips quirked. "Okay... go sit. I'll bring it out."

The older couples were on their way out, their dishes also left sitting out on the table. Bell grabbed himself one of the last clear tables and watched the kitchen witch behind the counter. They were alone in the shop, and rather than her tension ratcheting up, it was slowly dissipating. Either he was losing his edge, or he wasn't what bothered her.

She joined him at the table, a slice of quiche on one plate, and a cup and saucer of steaming, dark liquid in the other. Drinking chocolate. Bell's mouth watered. The chocolate croissant she had served him before had been a kind of decadence Hell only dreamed of, bitter and sweet, flaking and crisp on the outside and still warm and melting inside. The drinking chocolate was so much worse. It slid onto his tongue like a caress, spice immediately tickling the back of his throat. It was barely sweet, closer to coffee than chocolate, and he felt as though he was fighting a losing battle trying to keep himself from showing any enjoyment.

He was. He lost the battle, eyes sliding shut briefly. When they opened again, the witch was smug, relaxed in the chair across from his, her eyes bright with triumph. He ignored her and picked up the fork, digging into the quiche and taking a bite as if he could exorcise the delight of the chocolate.

He grunted. Damn her.

Fucking quiche was amazing. Salty and spicy sausage, sweet apple, acidic goat cheese. His stomach purred.

"Heavenly, isn't it?" she asked, laughter vibrating in her shoulders.

Damn her again, he wanted to smile. "Not sure the puritans above would approve," he said instead.

Which was a lie, but that was what he excelled at. Heaven would give its left nut to get its hands on Josie Benoit and her cooking. If he had a proper heart, it might have warmed from the tastes on his tongue alone. As it was, the one he'd invented was having a strange kind of spasm. Maybe she'd poisoned the chocolate.

"What are you and your *crew* doing in Sweet Pea?" she asked.

"Administrative work." Bell shrugged as she stared back at him, expression blank with disbelief. He took a slurping sip of the chocolate.

"I don't know if I believe your kind of administration doesn't include murder in its repertoire," she said, frowning down at the table, her fingertip tracing the swirling pattern of the formica.

It might, he thought. Before the end of their stay in Sweet Pea. They might not do the act itself, but it wouldn't mean they weren't the cause.

"And what about you, Cupcake? Where were you two nights ago?" He leaned forward, fork digging into the quiche, his tongue already anticipating its next taste, even as he tried to resist the pleasure of the flavors. "There's powerful magic in killing, for a witch that wants it."

"We protect this town," Josie said, dark eyes meeting his. He wanted to needle her to defensiveness, but all that frustration from earlier had melted away and her stare was clear on his face, a kind of penetration that raised his hackles. "If you're here, I guess that means we need to step our game up."

"You're outgunned," he said, and the words came out as a warning.

Josie only smiled. "You dunno who I got at my back, demon. Enjoy the food. It's on the house."

She pushed herself away from the table, flitting around him to bus and clean up after her customers. Music turned up over the speakers as she returned to her kitchen, a man's rasping voice singing a gospel song with a sinful beat to the drums and trilling trumpets. Josie's humor curled through the air with the music, prickling at his skin.

Bell was a demon who liked to keep a loose score in his mission: his successes and the occasional failures. He didn't appreciate that he was leaving this conversation without a clear sense of who had won. He took another deep sip of the chocolate in the small cup and realized—as bitter, rich liquid warmed him from head to toe—that this was indeed a defeat.

He cleared his table and took the dishes to the bussing station—scraped clean, because defeat or not, he wasn't wasting a bite. On the street outside, Chad Schmidt the businessman leaned against the driver's door of a luxury SUV, holding a conversation with what looked like the air until Bell realized the man had an ear piece in.

"Nah, not sure the deaths will be an issue. If it makes it to the national news, it'll just drive the price of the property down."

Bell grinned and shook his head, heading down the block back to the club. Chad Schmidt could've been one of Hell's finest if he'd wanted. That soul was already well and truly marked.

Inside the club, the crew was collected together around the narrow kitchen behind the bar, burgers cooking on the grill. As good as it smelled, Bell doubted it would measure up to the meal he'd just devoured.

"Danny cooks," Ashtaroth said.

Danny looked significantly less likely to faint at any moment around them as he stood behind the grill. "Mostly traditional Chinese from my gran, but I can flip burgers."

Burgers and Chinese food. Why not? "You know your way around a professional kitchen?" Bell asked.

"Worked at High Top through high school, but the manager is an ass," Danny said.

"Well, we're probably not much better, but the job is yours if you want it."

Danny's eyebrows rose, and Pie hummed in thought. "You want to run a restaurant? Bar too?" Pie asked.

"Just beer to start," Bell said. "We'll open late and see if we can pick up traffic from Gunney's. Or High Top's audience. Danny, find yourself some help in the kitchen."

"I want the bar," Barbie said, rough and simple.

Looked like there was a new candidate for least welcoming bartender in town.

"Call it Inferno Grill," Bell said. He looked to Pie and added, "Round out the details?"

His second nodded, and then blinked behind round glasses and leaned in Bell's direction. "You smell like butter."

Bell stretched his shoulders and crossed his arms over his chest. "Went to get food, didn't I?"

King Paimon the Great, raised one dark eyebrow. "You did."

"Burgers are ready," Danny chimed in. "We're gonna need waitresses. Unless...you guys are gonna..."

"No," Vinny said, glowering, and holding out a plate with a waiting bun.

10

FRIENDLY INTERVIEWS

Josie cursed as the ringtone started just as she parked in the guest lot of the country Sheriff's department. Either Mémé's sixth sense was working, or Josie's life was developing shit timing. Both seemed like the obvious answer.

"Heyyyy Mémé," Josie said, shutting off her car and staring at the front entry lights of the sheriff's office.

"'Lo dere, Piti bean," Mémé greeted. "Why ain't you callin' your Mémé no more?"

Piti bean, little bean.

"I was *just* picking the phone up," Josie said, smiling at the croak and roll of her grandmother's voice on the other end of the line. Mémé made a rude sound, and Josie's grin grew wider. She rested her head back against the seat of her car and closed her eyes.

"You sound dead tired, Piti." The 'r' in 'tired' turning into a long 'ya.'

"I'm a little worn out this week," Josie admitted. "How 'bout you?"

"Oh, you know, you know. Dees ol' bones got a lotta say nowadays. I won't complain."

Josie would have to call Auntie Nancy and get the truth out of that. Nancy was probably hearing plenty of complaints. And, truth be told, every time Josie saw Mémé's name on the caller ID of her cell, she felt a little wave of relief that she was still alive. She needed to get back down to New Orleans and see her grandmother before that wasn't the case.

"You hear from Ma?" Josie asked, voice getting small as her throat squeezed around the words.

Mémé sighed. "Not since Christmas, baby."

"Yeah. I got the birthday call last year." Ramona remembered her family every year in December, just in time to call Josie on her birthday and her mother on Christmas.

"She'll call ag'in dis year," Mémé said. "You good though?"

"I'm good," Josie said.

"You busy ain't you? Got no chat in you tonight."

Josie grimaced. "A little busy. But I've got time."

"Nah, nah. Just givin' you a ring. I'll say a word to de Ghedes for you, Piti."

"Same, Mémé," Josie said. Although, Mémé's words were probably better heard by the family saints than any prayer Josie gave them.

"Bissous," they chorused. *Kisses.* Josie blinked tears away as Mémé hung up. Nothing like taking a call from your grandmother before you had to have an interview with the local detectives about a murder.

Mark Nolan had made the call that afternoon, asking her to come down to the station for a 'friendly interview.' Which meant that the strange, fake ritual site they'd checked out in the woods was probably being looked at in connection with the murders. Josie was just getting out of her car when a familiar face walked out of the front doors of the station.

"June."

For a moment, June's stare was absent at the call of her name, before she took a deep breath and focused on Josie's face as they met on the sidewalk.

"I didn't tell them the athame was Imogen's," June whispered, eyes filling up with sudden tears.

The shock of seeing tears in June's eyes stunned Josie more than the confession of the lie. "Okay. Did Imogen tell you the bikers are demons?"

June's mouth remained open, thoughts spiraling in her head. "No," she said eventually.

Over June's shoulder, Mark Nolan waited in the lobby. "I need to get inside before they think we're colluding." They *were* colluding, but Josie was counting on Mark's minor infatuation with June to let them get away with it.

June nodded. "I'll... I'll talk to you soon."

Josie watched her friend hurry to her car, bouncing the heel of her foot against the sidewalk with worry. So they were lying to the detectives. That was never a recipe for success. Josie loved a good mystery story as much as the next person, but she wasn't feeling fond of being a potential suspect in the case. She made it to the door as Mark held it open for her.

"Hey Mark," she said, finding a smile.

"Hi Jo- Miss Benoit," Mark said, stumbling over her name as they turned and found two men in suits waiting for them. "This is Detective Bagley, and Sergeant Crowley," he said, pointing to the two middle-aged men.

Like Aleister Crowley, Josie thought glancing at the Sergeant. Except now was not the time to be referencing historical dark occult leaders. Bagley was the taller of the two, hair too long around his neck and receding too far back on the top of his head, little black wisps hanging on hopefully to the top of his head. Crowley looked about as un-occult as was possible, with the body of a retired football player. His forehead was dewy with sweat, gray hair sticking to his temples.

"Nice to meet you both," she said with a nod. Another lie.

"This way, Miss Benoit," Crowley said, and Bagley waited for her to walk forward before taking up the rear.

Pinned in. Faint panic rose up in her chest. *Quit actin' like a deer in the sights of gators,* Mémé's voice teased in her head.

"Aww, Josie," said Deputy Wallabey, a lovely old man who should've retired five years ago and seemed to be consigned to desk duty. "Didn't bring nothin' for us?"

"Next time," Josie said, shoulders relaxing as she passed his desk with a smile. She was herded down a hall and into a small room. There was a video camera in the right upper corner, and a wide table with a single seat facing two.

She took her spot at the table, facing off the investigators. She even managed a sincere smile as Detective Bagley reassured her that this was mostly an informational conversation since she'd been at the first scene, and gave her name for the record.

And then Crowley slid a folder across the table and flipped it open, revealing a photo, a selfie, of a young couple with their cheeks smashed together and huge, inebriated, smiles on their faces.

"Miss Benoit have you ever seen either of these people before?"

Aw shit.

"Yeah," Josie said, heaviness sinking in her chest. "They came into my bakery."

"When was that?"

She sighed, really not enjoying the beginning of this 'friendly interview.' "The day before they died," she said. And then, to clarify before they had to ask her to, "Thursday."

JUNE WAS WAITING on the inside steps of Josie's apartment when she got back home, and Josie gaped at her.

"Just tell me I left my door unlocked," Josie said, her brow furrowing.

June was a heap, wrapped up in an ivory sweater and huddled in on herself. She looked as if she might have been crying, or sleeping, or both, as she waited for Josie to come home.

"I broke in," June said softly. "I'm sorry. Did you tell them?"

"About Imogen's athame?" Josie asked. June nodded, and Josie released a long breath. "No. Come on. I'm hungry and we need to talk."

June shuffled off the step and waited for Josie to pass her before following up to the apartment. Josie opened the door into her living room, flipping the light switch. The small lamp by her couch turned on, blue scarf over its shade keeping the room cool and serene.

Not many people who met Josie outside of her home or work would've called her 'girly.' She had a uniform of black she preferred to wear, and it was too hot in a kitchen for her to grow her hair out into its natural curls. But the inside of her apartment was pastels and florals and soft browns. It was cozy, and sweet, and it made her feel at *home* when she walked in. After growing up with her mom, constantly changing apartments, it was a good feeling to have found herself growing into a space for five years, rather than packing it up every winter.

June crossed directly to the rounded chair by the window, curling into the cushion and grabbing the blanket off the back. Josie, faced with the crisis of June and the personal, raw feeling left after being interviewed by the detectives, did the one thing she'd always known seemed to offer comfort where it was needed. She went into her kitchen and looked for something to feed them both. The counter overlooked the living room—her bedroom was wonderfully spacious but the rest of the rooms ended up a little cramped—and Josie kept the rest of the lights off, choosing instead to light a small candle on the ledge of the half-wall between kitchen and living room.

June struck Josie as a woman who badly lacked for care in her life. Seeing June curled in on herself, paralyzed with the tangle of worries and fear reigning in her mind, she confirmed Josie's theory.

"Do you think Imogen killed those tourists?" What Josie did not excel at, was being delicate in her conversation.

"No," June said, looking up from where her fingers knotted together in her lap. "I don't believe that."

Josie nodded and set to cutting thick slices of carrot cake for each of them. Carrots were a vegetable so that was nutritious, right? If they were still hungry, she might be able to scrounge up something savory. The cake was landing on two mismatched porcelain plates when June spoke again.

"That doesn't mean she isn't responsible, though."

Josie sucked in a deep breath, blinked through the shock

of the revelation, and grabbed two forks. "Okay. How do you mean?" She crossed to the couch, sitting and tucking her legs beneath her before holding out one of the plates.

June took the cake and scratched patterns into cream cheese frosting with the tines of her fork as she chewed on the inside of her mouth, words building up in her chest. "If... if the circle we found in the woods was Imogen's. If she *brought* something here."

"Something like demons?" Josie asked, and June shrugged. Josie's eyebrows slid up. "Do you think that circle was hers?" June's brow furrowed and her lips pressed together, jaw working but no words coming out. For once, Josie could actually read her. June's instinct said 'no', that her sister was innocent, but June hated instinct. So Josie decided to throw her a bone. "I don't think it was Imogen."

Blonde hair flicked through the air with the force of June's head jerking up. "You don't?"

"No. I know Imogen could probably clean up after herself, but that girl has *juice* in her magic. And that circle? Pfft. There was *nothing*. It was dead. Convincing looking, but no energy."

June sagged back into the chair, finally taking a bite of cake. "Mark Nolan said they're looking at the two sites as connected. Bloody footprints in the same shoe size were found at both scenes. And a smaller set at the murder scene but they aren't sure if it was just a normal hiker from before the murder."

Josie coughed on her bite of cake. "Mark Nolan told you case information?"

"He wouldn't tell me the shoe sizes," June said, shrugging and taking a bite.

Was June oblivious or conniving, Josie wondered,

sucking frosting from her fork. It was impossible to tell. But the questions didn't end there.

"Okay so... Imogen. She recognized one of the bikers," Josie said, waiting for June to meet her eyes before continuing, "As a *demon*. Like...from Hell?"

Mémé had always said the dead, the dark souls of the world were left stuck on earth, and Josie believed this. She cleansed the homes she moved into, spoke respectfully of the dead, and tried not to let her occasional bad moods lead her to tip the scales in the wrong direction. She wanted to pass on peacefully, not end up stuck in the same old place for eternity.

Damn. Did that mean if she'd met demons from Hell it was time to convert?

"Imogen has always struggled with..." June trailed off and then took a deep breath. "She can work such strong magic. And for her, it's always been about whether or not she can work the magic, not *what* the magic is that she's cutting her teeth on. For about six years now she's been... she really has been trying to..."

Josie didn't use words like light and dark when it came to magic. Growing up with voodoo, and all the silly things people thought of the craft, she'd learned that most magic fell into a beautifully wide gray area. Imogen had that quality in her magic, and Josie had always been comfortable with the younger woman and her power.

"She said it happened before the coven formed," Josie reasoned, and June sighed and nodded.

"That makes sense. Wait. What are demons doing in Sweet Pea?" June's eyes were wide, glowing by the blue light of the lamp.

"That's my question! But whatever their reason, it didn't

have anything to do with Imogen. She was *pissed* when she ran into them."

"How many disasters are we dealing with, right now?" June breathed out.

Josie shrugged and took another bite. "Think they call this kind of situation a clusterfuck."

11  BANKS COUNTY CALLS A MEETING

Rosa had Josie's arm in a vice grip, pulling the petite woman through the crowd at the Banks County Municipal Hall, searching for June's familiar blonde head.

"You think everyone's really here to argue about whether or not to sell Merryweather, or just get rowdy about the murders?" Rosa asked. She tried to whisper, but Rosa didn't really do whispers and at least five heads turned in their direction to stare.

"Probably both," Josie admitted, and then managed a glimpse of June as someone sat down. She pulled back on her elbow, redirecting Rosa. "Over there. She's got sweaters on seats for us."

"Course she does. She runs cold blooded, that one."

Josie bit off the words in her mouth. June wasn't cold blooded. She was *restrained* that was for sure, but there was a beating heart in that thin chest, and it was absolutely devoted to her sister Imogen. But Rosa didn't know about the athame yet, and since Josie had settled on the coping method of denial—that there were demons in Sweet Pea, that she was a person of interest in a murder investigation, that she maybe-sort-of suspected Imogen of involvement— she didn't want to bring the topic up if she could help it.

"'Scuse us. Sorry. Just left our purses over here. Don't mind us. Yes, thank you for stretching your legs out Janet, that really helps," Rosa muttered, her bright orange boots stomping over and around ankles as the pair of them squeezed down the narrow row of chairs.

"Council really packed in the seats," Josie said, wincing as she stepped on someone's coat. She excused herself with the reassurance that that was what you got for not wadding it up on your lap.

June moved her sweaters off the chairs she reserved as they reached her, but her gaze was distant. "Sit down and look over there. See who else came tonight?"

Josie sat and followed June's stare. As if her eyes were magnetically drawn to him, she found Bell on the far end of the County court auditorium, he and his crew propped against the wall like a pack of bouncers at a bar.

"What do they care about *Merryweather*?" Rosa said, leaning forward to stare. "Oh lord, I know they're bad— they're bad right? But even my abuelita would make eyes at those men, and she is a living saint. Oh! I know! Maybe they're here *because* of Merryweather. Maybe it's like a... a hell mouth?"

"Yeah okay, Buffy," Josie said, lips cracking into a smile. Bell caught her stare then, and she jerked back in her seat, staring up at the empty council table at the front of the room.

"Hell mouths aren't real," June said, which Josie found relieving until the other woman continued, "Demons can be accessed from our world, and access our world, from anywhere."

Which was just not very comforting.

"Demons can access my bed," Rosa whispered, laughing. She cleared her throat. "Just kidding. They're evil, right?"

"They're demons," Josie said shrugging. "I don't think they're here to beautify the neighborhood." And as if she'd read Rosa's mind—because the demons, men, *were* beautiful—she hissed, "Oh, just hush."

"You said they claimed they weren't responsible for the murders?" June asked.

Josie and Rosa both nodded, and Josie found herself turning to look at Bell again. He was watching her, an almost invisible smile on his face and just enough warmth in his stare for her cheeks to threaten to blush.

"But they could've been lying," Josie said, lifting her chin.

"You didn't have them in a sacred circle, so they aren't bound to tell you the truth," June agreed.

"Just so you know, we are getting some looks," Rosa whispered.

Sure enough, when Josie tore her stare off Bell she found a few people in seats nearby giving them curious stares for their conversation. *Serves you for eavesdropping*, she thought to them.

Thankfully, at the same moment, the lights dimmed slightly in the auditorium, and the heavy buzz of conversation dulled around the room. County council members hurried up to the table on stage where microphones sat in front of the center three seats. At the center of the group, County Commissioner Laila Wilson took her seat. She'd been the Mayor of Sweet Pea when Josie first arrived, and while everyone in town called her a 'hard ass,' it was said with a hearty amount of respect. They'd had figurehead mayors in Sweet Pea plenty of terms before. Laila Wilson may have been an elegant and attractive woman, red hair streaked with fading gray blonde always twisted up off her long neck, but she promised to work and she'd followed through on the vow.

"Our first order of business is always to thank you all for coming out, supporting Banks County and its members of government in doing their best to serve you. We have a packed house tonight, and we'd like to remind everyone that while we always take open questions at the end of the night, the order of business for this meeting is *only* to discuss the upcoming vote on the sale of Merryweather Nature Preserve. Any questions regarding the ongoing investigation will, please, need to be held until the end of the evening." Commissioner Wilson's voice raised in volume slowly during the announcement as the rumble of protest rose up from around the auditorium.

"Is the investigation looking for a local suspect?" someone shouted from the opposite side of the room.

Rosa huffed and whispered, "Sir, did you not hear the woman?" She was an avid Laila Wilson fan after the former mayor made a regular weekly order of bouquets to her home when Rosa opened her florist business, Flora Fresca.

"Here we go," Josie breathed as the volume of the room rose.

There was no hope of hearing an answer from the council, not over the rabble of conversation that followed the man's question. A gavel banged from one of the podiums and Josie caught a brief eye roll from Wilson, whose hand raised, waiting for quiet like a second grade teacher who knew only a look would quell the riot. Slowly the noise softened, and only when there was a remaining hush of whispers, did Wilson finally lean forward to speak.

"The investigators will hold a local press conference tomorrow, sharing what they are able to then. Tonight, we are hearing *only* arguments on the sale of Merryweather Nature Preserve, for and against." Her eyes searched the crowd and before the roar of questions rose again she pointed to the back of the room. "Richard Merryweather. Why don't you start us off?"

"Oh she's good," Rosa said, and Josie nodded.

It was a genius tactic. The only thing that was even remotely interesting under the shockwave of the recent murders would be the reaction of the last Merryweather on the sale of land they had gifted to the county only decades ago. One of Wilson's fellow commissioners shot her a glare, and Josie thought maybe there had been some previous hope of keeping Richard from speaking up. It did the trick, though. As Richard Merryweather walked up the narrow aisle to the microphone waiting at the front of the room, the audience settled.

Josie hadn't totally made her mind up when it came to the sale of the preserve. She knew Rosa was in favor. A great hotel settled within the scenic hikes of the area would bring destination weddings, and those weddings would bring business. No one would ship in flowers when Rosa's work was already perfection. Josie would probably land a fair amount of trade from that too if she wanted, although wedding cakes weren't her preferred bake. Business aside, she hated to think of the forest being rearranged and ripped out, even if it might keep Sweet Pea and the surrounding towns thriving on visitors. Listening to Richard Merryweather might sway her vote to keep the preserve out of sale, if she couldn't make up her mind on her own.

He tugged at the sleeves of his too-large suit coat as he

stepped up to the microphone, one hand reaching up to briefly sweep over the top of his hair, reminding Josie of a high school boy about to have his picture taken. He looked to be about in his early fifties, a sort of average kind of attractive, and she knew from local gossip that he was the last of the Merryweathers, living on the remaining family property just west of the preserve. He cleared his throat twice before speaking and Josie found herself wishing him a little good luck.

"M-my family, we were some of the first trappers in this region. We gained a lot of land for the growing communities—"

"From the native peoples," Rosa muttered.

"A lot of trade. Good farming. And we were never ones to… to plaster our names on things. Didn't run for offices. Didn't try to tell nobody how to live. Just did our best to make this a good place for everybody to settle." He had a piece of paper in his hand, crumpled, which he glanced down to frequently without really seeming to read from it.

"We had lots of offers to log those hills, but my granddad always thought that would just take the spirit of the country right out of the land to do that. And maybe we weren't smart or careful enough, but I guess my family just assumed that when they gifted the land to the county, it would be accepted in the spirit it was meant. As a… a gesture of *trust,* and of y'all knowing what it was worth. I don't think Everett Merryweather ever woulda gifted you these hills if he'd known that worth would be summed up in dollar signs. So since I gotta say this, I'll say it. Vote No on the sale of Merryweather Preserve next month. Th-thank you."

The applause rose slowly through the room, and Josie felt Rosa squirm uncomfortably in the seat next to her. Friendly support aside, Josie's resolve was made and she let her own hands join in support of Richard Merryweather as he made a slow retreat to the back of the room.

"I was gonna speak but now..." Rosa grimaced and shrugged. "I still think the sale would benefit the town."

Josie shrugged. Maybe it would and maybe it would just be a shopping complex or a hotel or some kind of gimmicky trail-adventure business. She'd vote for the preserve instead. In fact, it seemed as though everyone was having trouble working up the courage to speak up after Merryweather.

A hard elbow jabbed into Josie's ribs and she jumped in her seat, twisting to face June. "Watch," June whispered, nodding her head to the other side of the room.

One of the bikers—it took Josie a minute to remember, but it was the big redhead named Vinny—paced down the length of the room and then crouched down at the corner of the seated area. A moment later a tall woman with a swinging blonde ponytail and eyeshadow up to her eyebrows, stood from her seat in the center of the pack, and marched up to the microphone, taking it in trembling hands with long electric blue nails.

"All due respect," the woman began, and Josie's fingers wrapped around the seat of her chair, bracing for impact. "But I'm from Damsville, just opposite little Sweet Pea on the preserve, and it took me *twenty* minutes to drive here tonight. There's not a single highway within ten minutes of Damsville, which means we see zilch of the tourist traffic. Our businesses have been withering for those same decades that Merryweather's been in the county's hands."

A cheer rose up from the corner of the room where the woman had been sitting, and Josie turned to watch Vinny slide back against the wall amongst the other demons.

"What's it say that the demons are lobbying for sale of

the preserve?" Josie whispered, studying the seven men along the wall.

"Welllll shiiit," Rosa sighed, and slumped in her seat.

Bell caught Josie's gaze again, one eye winking at her.

"It says we need to find out why," June answered.

12 · HOUSE GUESTS

"You want to do *what*?" Imogen asked them.

June, Rosa, and Josie were crowded together on the top step of Imogen's porch, the house dark behind the woman blocking their way through the door.

"Summon a demon," Josie repeated.

Imogen's stare turned to focus on June. "You aren't serious."

"We are," June said.

The sisters stared at one another, and Josie couldn't tell if they were reading each other's thoughts, or if they were so in tune that they could communicate beyond even facial expressions by now. Josie burrowed deeper into her hoodie, waiting for the silent conversation to complete. She hoped Imogen made up her mind and had the heat running inside. October was coming in with a mean cold streak this year.

"Don't you want to know why there are demons in Sweet Pea?" Rosa asked, and when Imogen's gaze flicked in her direction, she added with a light barb in her tone, "Ones you *didn't* summon."

"Come in," Imogen said, shoulders sagging with a sigh as she stepped back, pulling the door open wide at her side.

June entered first, fumbling on the inside wall until a light came on. Josie had never been inside Imogen's house before, and she wasn't sure what to expect. Something like June's cozy and tidy clutter in clean colors maybe, or spaces that were all mysterious and dark. In reality, the open living area she walked into was nothing like Imogen at all; the log walls and dark curtains were dusty and the furniture was dated. It reminded Josie of a cabin she and her mom had rented once in the upper peninsula of Michigan for a summer, where Josie had slept on a lumpy pull-out couch underneath a ceiling fan that wobbled dangerously while it ran.

Imogen's kitchen was worse. All the appliances had to be the ones originally installed with the cabin, and they didn't look as though they saw much use. Josie knew June and Imogen had inherited the cabin from their parents when they were still teenagers, and that after a few years in foster care the sisters had returned to live there. June moved out to her own apartment shortly before Josie arrived in town. Five years later, and Josie suspected the house looked essentially the same as it had when their parents were alive. Josie knew Imogen was a writer, had published a successful book of essays on witchcraft years ago, but she never heard of any current project. There was no evidence anywhere in the cabin of how Imogen lived, day to day, aside from the remnants of a pot of coffee sitting on the counter.

Imogen shut the door behind them and stood in place, looking like she might be considering running out, her hands fidgeting in front of her as June helped herself to turning on lamps. June stopped in front of the couch where a pile of books were spread out over a low coffee table, dinged and stained with age. She lifted a thin, weathered leather-bound book up from the pile, frown furrowing her brow as she read the page.

"You're researching them," June said, looking up from the book to Imogen.

"I wanted to know which of them were here," Imogen said.

Josie felt as though she and Rosa could've walked right out of the cabin, and neither of the sisters would have noticed. She cleared her throat and waited for Imogen to look at her. "Did you figure it out?"

"I think so," Imogen said, nodding. She tugged at the cuffs of her sweater and crossed the room, taking the book from June's hands. "Rosa gave me the names they're using, and they aren't great disguises. They weren't expecting to be discovered."

Rosa smiled at the news and went to sit on her knees in front of the table. "Okay, so who do we have?"

June and Imogen sat on the couch, and Josie joined Rosa on the floor, the book open between them. Josie's lips twitched as she noticed the electric green sticky notes Imogen had used to mark the pages, contrasting harshly against the frail pages, yellow with age.

"Beleth, King of Hell," Imogen said, flicking to the first tab.

"King?" Josie asked, eyebrows raising. "This is...Bell? Mr. Bad News?"

Imogen smiled. "That's...an appropriate name for him. And he's *a* King. Hell has quite a few, but he's definitely a notable one. Specializes in war, strategy, and the sexual satisfaction of the conjurer."

Josie choked on air, horrified by the blush rising up her cheeks. Rosa cackled after one look at her, but the sisters at least seemed to miss the joke. There went all Josie's weak determination to believe that Bell wouldn't be worth the trouble he might bring with him.

"And the one called Ash?" June asked.

"Ashtaroth," Imogen said. "He's... interesting. Not one of Hell's royalty, but not a lower demon either. Specializes in mathematics and handicrafts."

Rosa's laugh grew breathless at this description. "I'm sorry," she gasped. "Did you just say the demon of *handicrafts*? Like...are we sure these guys aren't just fairies?"

"The fae are an entirely different breed of trouble," Imogen said with a completely straight face.

"Wait. Wait, so. Fae, demon... this isn't ruling each other out?" Josie asked, perking up. "And the Loa."

Imogen shrugged. "As far as I'm aware, most of these mythologies exist. You have experience with the Loa?"

Josie nodded slowly, but raised a hand in the air, wobbling it side to side. "I was at ceremonies when I was young. I saw the possessions of Loa spirits take my family, but... I guess finding out demons existed too sort of shook my certainty that what I believed was real."

Imogen hummed, eyes distant with thought. "I think belief lends to reality. I feel the strength at your altars to your spirits. You aren't feeding into nothing."

Josie sighed and nodded. So it was all just one big tangle of spiritualities then. She didn't mind that, she liked the lane she'd grown up in, and the one she'd found with her coven. Now she just needed to figure out how to keep this new world of demons from harming the world she loved.

"So one King, and one crafty demon," Rosa said, snorting at her joke. "Who else we got?"

"Two more Kings, Paimon and Vine."

"Pie and Vinny," Josie said, thinking of the ice blond with the glasses, and the redheaded monster.

"Three Kings seems like..." June trailed off, lips twisting in a frown.

"Heavyweights for Sweet Pea," Imogen finished, staring at her sister. "I agree. The others, Aim and Barbatos, are Dukes, dangerous in their own right. Dantalion is a Duke, too. The one who concerns me most is Vine. One, he's not a fan of witches, and two, he can steal souls without permission."

"Demons require permission to steal souls?" Rosa asked.

"It's a fairly organized hierarchy," Imogen said. "Even if Hell's goals are at opposite odds with Heaven's, they still operate within each other's parameters. According to the text, the permission to take a soul comes from up above."

"Vinny's the one who made me the most nervous," Josie admitted. "He looks like he's about two seconds from losing interest in playing human and taking out the whole town."

"He's dangerous. He's also the one most likely to cough up the answers you want," Imogen said, the warning clear in her voice as she looked at each of them.

"Why can't we call the low key one? Ashtaroth?" Rosa asked.

"Information isn't his domain," Imogen said with a shrug. "And if we think of these demons in terms of an army, which I think they might be with Beleth at the helm, a demon without rank is less likely to know as much as a King."

"Is it safe?" June asked.

Imogen went still, staring at the book on the table, eyes flicking over the words. Finally, she shook her head. "No. There's four of us, which is better protection, but you'll have to be very careful to do things exactly as I say. If he isn't bound properly, we won't get the answers, and we'll be trapped with a pissed off demon."

Josie was liking this plan less and less the longer she thought it through. It had seemed easy enough before hearing their names and ranks. What was so scary about a demon named Pie? King Paimon, on the other hand, had a weight on her tongue, and his sigil printed in the occult book looked cryptic and dizzying. "What about after? We're not talking about summoning a demon from Hell, and then sending them back. What happens when we run into this guy on the street again?"

"Demons are bound by strict rules. Being invoked is a contract they're required to perform when called on. Provided we don't break any rules, they can't act against us," Imogen said. "But that doesn't mean it's safe. Not just in the act. We don't know why they're here yet. If their orders include us as collateral damage, then that's what we'll be."

"That's true, even if we don't demand answers," June said. She and Imogen locked gazes again, and Josie wished they would share with the class for once.

"You still want to? Really?" Imogen whispered.

Rosa sat up straight, sliding the book to herself and turning back to Vine's pages. "Sweet Pea is my home. I wanna know what I gotta do to keep it safe. So you two better make up your minds and help, so I don't get eaten by an angry demon."

ACCORDING TO IMOGEN, there were five concrete elements of demon summoning, and then a sixth—intention, which was the most important. As rituals went, Josie found it to be surprisingly similar to many others she'd participated in, including calling the Loa. It took a day to prepare before they returned to Imogen's cabin, where she led them downstairs to the basement. Then down another, more narrow, set of stairs that led to a dark, empty, and stifling cellar. There was a chalk circle that took up seventy-five percent of the floor, leaving tight corners for each of the witches to stand in.

Rosa was kneeling by a large incense burner, dressed in a simple black sheath dress they had each purchased for the ritual, something new and uncluttered with daily energy. She packed the burner with wormwood and dandelion, and some fresh tobacco that Josie thought Ghede Linto would've approved of based on the pungent stench. Josie arranged a plate of nearly raw deer meat she'd purchased from a local hunter, and a cracked pomegranate. June had a pair of hand cymbals in her grip, her knuckles white around the handles as she watched her sister finish painting a gold disk with a white sigil, Vine's mark.

"Are you ready?" Imogen murmured, brush poised to make the final lines. Josie thought Vine's sigil looked a little like a man's face wearing a crown, arrows coming down from the crown.

"Ready," Rosa said, bouncing on her toes.

June nodded, and Imogen looked to Josie last. "Ready," Josie said, voice cracking with nerves.

"Whatever happens, keep your feet where they are. Don't smudge the circle," Imogen instructed.

The coven nodded, and the brush landed on gold, an inverted crown marking down the line of the empty face. Imogen set the gold seal on the floor at the northwestern corner of the circle and rose up, candle flames around the circle stretching waist-high with her movement.

Josie swallowed, her throat tight and the temperature in

the room flaring warmer. Her sheath dress scratched at her hips, just a hair too snug over her curves. Her palms sweat against the porcelain of the plate in her hand. She tried to quell the thunderous racing of her heart, but as Imogen's hands raised to her sides, palms up, Josie's heart only hammered faster.

What a dumb idea, Josie thought. Except it had been hers.

"Thee I invoke, Vine, child of the Bornless one," Imogen called, her voice drawing up the same weight and command Josie had first heard on the street outside of Rosa's, as Imogen threatened a pack of demons.

"Thee, who makes home in the void place,

Thee, who steals souls without granting,

Thee, who tears walls and builds towers,

Thee, of rough waters and great storms,

Thee, who sees my kind in their hiding."

Rosa's breath caught audibly as the candle flames wavered and sputtered as the air grew damp and thick with the ozone of an approaching storm. Imogen nodded to them, the circle was working, hooking into the demon Vine wherever he was, tugging him to them.

"Hear me, Vine,

Ar thiao rheibet atheleberseth,

A blatha abeu ebeu phi,

Thitasoe ib thiao."

Josie shivered at the eerie sounds on Imogen's tongue, and when she looked to June, her gray eyes were pressed shut, a shimmer of tears on her cheeks. Imogen continued, calling Vine again and reciting his skills and accolades, before repeating the eerie chant. An impossible breeze circled the sealed room, and Josie had to fight to keep still as the candle flames licked at her sides, threatening to catch.

"Come thou, into the circle.

Come, Vine, and hear my command.

Come and obey my will to which you are bound into keeping.

These are the words!" Imogen bellowed, eyes focused hard on the center of the chalk circle.

The air wavered there in the heart of the circle, smoke from the burner catching on the breeze and spiraling into the center of the room, until it formed a heavy cloud.

"He's coming," Imogen whispered, and her eyes were huge and wild, fixed with hunger on the growing smoke.

The weight of the room grew crushing, as if the ground was dragging Josie down, her knees wobbling beneath the dress she wore. She understood as she watched, the smoke stretching and contorting until it was formed into a beastly shape, shadows darkening behind the pale gray cloud of perfumed smoke. The rumble of tension and magic expanded into a blaring roar, a growl trumpeting with rage. The floor shook, and Josie locked her knees and held her breath as her eyes watered, the heat too strong and the smoke too fragrant.

June's cymbals came together with a crash on the opposite side of the room, out of Josie's sight, and the tremble in the ground stopped. Smoke sank to the floor, and the growl softened to a low and steady threat.

Josie's entire body was frozen as she stared at the demon they had trapped in the circle. It was not the redheaded beast of a man covered in tattoos and leather, but a tall and stocky figure seated atop an enormous black horse, whose gold hooves beat at the ground. It was impossible for the man and the horse to be as large as they were, to force Josie to stare up at them in terror. The ceiling was barely three feet above her own head but she felt as if she gazed up miles to look at Vine on the back of his steed.

He had a lion's head, blood red hair hanging down to the middle of his back, and eyes layers and layers of black above a snarling maw. He was naked, skin the shade of a vicious sunburn, and as he shifted on the horse, Josie caught sight of his cock, horrifyingly thick and short and angrily purple. *This* was the demon they'd called. The man who'd glowered and stomped through Sweet Pea was an illusion, and Josie was cowed to realize how comparatively friendly Vinny looked next to King Vine.

"Vine, King and Earl of Hell, you are bound to speak a true answer to the questions posed to you," Imogen said, and Josie marveled that the witch could bear to look directly into the demon's eyes.

"Witch, you are bound to die with my boot on your throat," Vine snarled back.

June stiffened, and the cymbals made a soft hissing rattle. Vine twitched and snarled, his head rolling on his shoulders in response to the sound.

Josie found Rosa's eyes where she stood in the corner to the right, and Rosa mouthed to her, "The fuck!"

"Why have you come to Sweet Pea?" Imogen asked.

"I was ordered to," Vine said, furred cheeks twitching and black eyes narrowing.

"What orders?"

"King Beleth the Warlord's."

"State them," Imogen said, snapping.

Vine snarled with irritation, and shifted again, the horse beneath him stepping back and forth in the scant inch of space inside the circle. "Be patient, Vinny," Vine said, but the voice was not his own. It was Bell's, sounding irritated and tired, the whisper rasp having the strange effect on Josie of unravelling some of the terror coiled in her chest. "Don't fucking touch that... Just wait... Just go do something fucking useful, would you?"

Imogen only smirked, and Josie wished she could speak. But she wasn't sure if that would break the invocation contract, and she wasn't about to face this lion headed demon in the tiny cellar. Imogen was quiet for a long stretch, in a staring contest with Vine, as she worked through the words.

"What is the intention of the Hell's Bells Motorcycle club in coming to Sweet Pea?"

Vine grumbled, the noise vibrating uncomfortable in Josie's ear. "To ruin this fucking town."

"How?"

"Whatever means necessary."

"Was it one of you that murdered the tourists in the woods?"

"... No," Vine admitted reluctantly.

Josie's eyes darted between them, and Imogen's own stare flicked to her. Josie's lips parted, a question crawling up her throat, and Imogen nodded.

"Why Sweet Pea?" Josie asked.

Vine's spine stiffened, and he tugged at the inky mane of his horse, the beast taking side steps to turn and face her. The breath on her face was painfully hot and dry and rancid as she stared up the long nose of the horse and into the lion's eyes.

"Shoulda had her start with the questions," Vine said, a black tongue flicking out over white fangs.

"Answer," Imogen commanded.

"Hell sent us here because on the map of the world, Sweet Pea is a fucking beacon of good," Vine said. "And it's bleeding into the earth and the people who live here. If we hadn't come, it might spread further."

His eyes, so electric and violent even in the darkest shade, were fastened to Josie's. She thought her own might burn up in her face before he released her stare. The longer she looked at him, the harder it was to breathe, to stand, to think. His voice pounded in her ears like a nail driving into a coffin.

"But we are here. And we will stomp this candy coated fucking shithole into embers and ash, and nothing beautiful will ever grow in this town, ever again. Four witches won't stop us. Nothing will."

June slammed the cymbals together with a crash, and lightning ribboned through the room, snapping down on Vine and his horse. The sound cracked, breaking the hypnotic pain of Vine's speech, and light blinded Josie, a slam of energy throwing her back into the wall behind her. Her head hit the stone, but the stab of pain was a relief in comparison to being trapped in Vine's gaze.

When the stars cleared from in front of her eyes, the candles had dimmed to blue wisps on small stubs of wax, and they were alone in the cellar of the cabin again. Rosa was seated on the floor, gasping for breath, and June had her arms around Imogen, supporting her younger sister as she sagged with exhaustion.

"What... what are we supposed to do?" Josie whispered, staring at the circle on the floor, the chalk scorched in the center.

"We protect Sweet Pea," June said, voice hard and eyes on her sister.

13   MISCALCULATIONS

Bell was waiting in the armchair of Vinny's bedroom, face turned down in a frown as he drummed his fingers on the leather in the idle minutes until the other demon reappeared. They'd been riding back to Grimsby House when the quiet stretch of street filled with the perfume of tangy herbs and tobacco. Vinny had barely pulled his bike over, when he snarled and leaped off the back into thin air. Bell had circled back to the spot, catching the last whiff of cinnamon and something floral.

The witches had snatched his soldier right out from under his nose.

In his mind, Bell kept his grip tight around the reins he'd been granted for the mission, waiting to feel slack on the line connecting him to Vinny. The thread loosened and Bell grinned, yanking hard on the leash.

Vinny was dragged to him, still snarling, body naked and twisted, lion's snarl bared.

"Control yourself," Bell ordered.

Vinny crouched and roared at Bell, his breath heavy with rot. Bell raised a hand, and the sound croaked to nothing. Vinny stumbled back on his heels and turned away, and Bell waited for the subtle shift, the demon standing taller and smoother. A moment later, re-dressed and with the human disguise in place, Vinny faced him again, and Bell released the stranglehold on his voice.

"You could have intervened," Vinny growled.

He should have intervened. Bell didn't want to admit that he hadn't expected the attack. He was chosen to lead this mission for a reason, and the moment they'd walked into Josie's bakery and found a witch, he should have been preparing for this moment. Instead, he found an excuse.

"I was curious. What did they want?" Bell said.

"To know why we're here," Vinny said, scuffing his hand through his bright hair and walking backwards to the foot of his bed. He'd claimed one of the guest bedrooms, immediately turning all the art to face the walls and taking every decorative knickknack and locking it in the closet. At least he hadn't burnt cigarette holes in the rose carvings of the headboard yet. It was Bell's personal opinion that petty vandalism was beneath their work.

"And did you tell them?" Bell asked.

Vinny bared his teeth at him. "You know how the contract works." So, yeah. The witches were aware. "For fucks sake, why are you smiling?" Vinny asked.

"I think this is going to be fun," Bell said, shrugging.

"We're compromised," Vinny said, slowing down his words as if Bell was missing the point.

He wasn't. Bell sighed and pushed up out of the chair, Vinny tensing on the bed. "If you're concerned about your chances against the witches, I can assure you that this team has everything under control," Bell said, smug smile spreading as Vinny glowered up at him. "It's been a long time since I've faced an actual opponent in battle. Sounds like an entertaining change in the plan."

Bell turned to let himself out, and Vinny's voice stopped him. "Would Curson agree? Or Morningstar?"

Bell's teeth ground in his jaw, but he smiled at Vinny as he turned. "Notify them, Vine. But it won't get you that transfer you requested. You were sent here to follow orders, *my* orders. Curson may have assigned you to this unit, but we are here on Morningstar's command. And if you think I haven't earned Morningstar's trust after my lifetime of service, you don't understand our master."

Bell left Vinny in the ensuing silence, taking the broad curling staircase downstairs. Privately, he wished Vinny's request to be transferred to a different mission had been granted. He didn't mind having another King on the mission, in fact he was glad to have Pie. Vinny was just an asshole, and Bell had a low tolerance for those. Pie had caught wind of the request after it'd been rejected, while Vinny was bitching to an indifferent Barbie.

Speaking of the taciturn demon, Aim and Barbie were in the kitchen burning something on the stove, the back door hanging open. Pie was in the garden, stretched out on a loveseat by the ironwork tea table, his head thrown back and eyes staring unfocused up at the stars. His glasses lay discarded on the table next to a cigarette burning in a porcelain saucer.

"Are you gonna smoke that?"

Pie blinked but didn't stir. "I just like the smell. Reminds me of offerings."

"Too bad the witches didn't summon you," Bell said, eyeing his second.

Pie hummed in something that might have been agreement. "They know now."

"Yes."

"Is this intentional or a miscalculation, Beleth?"

Bell huffed and threw himself into a chair on the opposite side of the table. "Does it have to be one of the two? Can't it be...convenient?"

"Will you retaliate?" Pie turned his head, and the smoke curling through the air between them twirled at the command of Pie's fingertip.

Bell grinned at the thought. "Well, I'll have to, won't I? Remind them who they're dealing with."

He ignored Paimon's narrow-eyed stare as the possibilities grew in his head. He knew just where to start.

THE KITCHEN WITCH'S home smelled like her, sweet and spicy, vanilla hanging like a cloudy backdrop over every piece of furniture. The apartment had a warmth to it that made Bell uneasy, as if those oversized pastel pink pillows on the couch were capable of dragging him into their depths and putting him into a lazy, decadent nap.

He helped himself to snooping through the living room first, rifling through magazines and notes on recipes. When that was dull and fruitless, he hunted the kitchen and discovered the world's most intensely chocolate brownies he'd ever tasted. There was magic in the kitchen, lingering on cupboard doors, but it was harmless and loving, only the intention of sharing care and kindness. Not even a damn love potion in sight.

The bedroom was a large open space with an enormous bed on a white platform. Beleth stared at the twisted sheets for longer than he would've cared to admit. Perhaps the man's body he was wearing was starting to develop a man's appetites, because he enjoyed the image of Josie his mind conjured, tan skin against baby blue sheets, curves on display. The reverie ended as a hum of power thrummed out of the corner of his left eye.

"Here we go," Bell purred, facing the altar arranged on a table in front of a large window.

He frowned as he stepped closer. It was unlike any altar he'd seen before. Witches' altars were meant to be tidy displays, made of natural items. The one in Josie's bedroom was cluttered and colorful, full of bottles of booze and a box of cigars, dry and fresh flowers, silk patterned scarves, a harmonica and a plastic tambourine, colorful drawings, and strange figurines that were a cross between saints and demons. Candles glowed in safe containers, and ash lay on an incense burner from the morning. Bell couldn't puzzle it out, but there was no denying the hearty glow that touched every single item on the table. Whatever Josie was praying to, it was listening.

Downstairs the front door shut, and Bell gave the altar a last look before heading back out into the living room. He propped himself against a supporting beam by the kitchen and waited for Josie to find him.

She came in with flour stains on her black clothes, and handprints on her hips that he wanted to cover with his own. She sighed and Bell grinned, waiting for her to turn and face him, to scream, for her heart to pound so loud in her chest he could hear it in his own veins.

"Have you been waiting long?"

His foot landed too hard against the wood floor as he shifted to stand straight, lips turning down in a scowl as Josie turned to face him. She raised her eyebrows, waiting for his answer.

"I didn't feel a ward," he said.

"So you thought I wouldn't notice you walking around? Directly over my own damn head," she said, crossing her arms over her chest. His stare pulled down to where her breasts pressed together.

Miscalculation, Pie's voice echoed in his head.

"You heard me?" he asked.

"No. But you've got a... heaviness on you. Gave me a damn headache," she muttered, rolling her head on her shoulders. "What do you want?"

How was... How was she *always* managing to put him just ever so slightly off balance? Bell's hackles raised on the back of his neck, and he dimmed the illusion clinging to his skin. Josie's eyes widened, and she stilled in front of him. *Good,* he thought. *Good. She should've been scared from the beginning.*

He embraced that heaviness she spoke of as he stepped closer to her, his boots hitting the floor like thunder, boards trembling beneath her feet. She barely cleared his chest, and he caught the slight hitching of her breath as he towered over her. He wondered how he looked this way, to her. Were his eyes glowing red? His fangs showing? She looked smaller, and he had an irritating urge to dig his fingers into her hips and draw her up to her tiptoes.

"If you wanted answers, you should have summoned *me*, Cupcake," Beleth said, and the words rattled in his throat. "I'm in charge, you know that."

"Are you saying you're jealous?" Josie asked. Her eyes were huge, and her voice shook. She was *terrified,* and she was still a little smart ass.

He let himself grin because he knew his smile at least would be fearsome. "I told you, we didn't murder your tourists."

"You did say that," Josie nodded, looking up at him from

under thick lashes. "And I didn't believe you. Are you surprised?"

Disappointed. He batted the thought away.

"What do you want Beleth?"

He had to freeze to keep from shivering. Had she just…? No. There was no magic in his name, no summons or contract, it was just the sound of it on her tongue. *Miscalculation.*

"Stay away from my men," Bell growled.

Josie was relaxing the longer they stood together, as if she was becoming immune to his intimidation. She shrugged. "Fine. But tell them that. Tweedle Dee and Tweedle Deranged were just in the shop buying eclairs. By the way, one of you should teach them about currency, or tell them to pick a foreign accent because they did not make a convincing argument for knowing how money works."

Shit. Aim and Barbie had been in her shop? Bell should've declared it off limits days ago. *But why*?

"Do you want to know who *did* kill the tourists?" Josie asked, her head tilting.

Bell took a step back. He was losing this argument, if it could even be called that. He didn't care about the tourists, or even the murderer if he was honest, but that wasn't what he said. "What do you mean?"

Josie slid around his side, and Bell's human illusion snapped back into place as he turned to watch her. She crossed to her kitchen, and he noticed that she seemed lighter here in her apartment, hips swaying in a way he found difficult *not* to watch.

"I'm gonna call on… an old friend of the family," Josie said, words hedging around their meaning. "Do you wanna come?"

Bell ground his jaw to keep from gaping at her. "We're on

the opposite sides of this fight, Cupcake."

"What fight?" Josie asked, packing those rich brownies into a plastic container. She looked up at him with wide eyes. "Oh. You mean Sweet Pea? Sure. If you wanna call it that."

His eyes narrowed, and he tried to stay focused as she turned and rose up on her tiptoes, stretching for a jar of something dark in a top cupboard. A sliver of skin peeked out between her t-shirt and jeans, and his mouth watered.

"You think we can't do it? Destroy this town?"

She grabbed a bottle of rum, hummed in thought, and then a bottle of whiskey. "You came to Sweet Pea, and within days there was a murder. There's never been a murder here before, did you know that? So yeah," she said, facing him again. "I think you can destroy the good in Sweet Pea. But since it wasn't you or your men that murdered those tourists, that means it was someone else, and I intend on finding out who. Would you like to come with me?"

He had no reason to say yes. It served no purpose to him to know, and despite what Josie said, he knew that whoever the murderer was, it wasn't his men that planted the seed. And despite the murder, Sweet Pea was still *shining* as if it had never been touched by a cloudy day in all its life.

"Where are we going?" he asked instead.

"To the woods," Josie said, shrugging.

Bell huffed. "You wanna summon spirits?"

That was a damn waste of time. And the only other beings he knew who she might call... they wouldn't be inclined to help and he wouldn't want them to see him with her.

Josie's lips curled and twitched with laughter. "Something like that. If he'll come. It's a long trip, so we'll see. Hey. Can we take your bike?"

14

A VISIT WITH PAPA LEGBA

Josie was ashamed to admit it, but her attraction to Bell just about doubled after climbing onto the back of his bike. She was fully in trouble when it came to this man. To this *demon*, she reminded herself. Even knowing so, she closed her eyes and savored the warmth of his thighs against the inside of hers, and the thrum of the engine beneath them. Bell's chest was firm beneath her grip on him, and she leaned into him as he handled a curve in the road, tipping the bike. It was cold out but Bell shed heat even through his jacket, and he was large enough that he blocked the wind from really hitting Josie at all.

This is just for the sake of a fantasy, she reassured herself. Except she had no reason to take him to the crossroads with her. She didn't know if she could call Papa Legba—the Loa spirit of the underworld and crossroads—on her own, and having Bell along might hinder that. Or it might help. Maybe Legba would be curious at the taste of a demon on the air with her. She smirked, her cheek pressed to the back of Bell's leather jacket, as she wondered how the demon would react if he knew he was one of her offerings to the Loa.

They arrived at the northern entrance of the park. The Sweet Pea entrance was too close to Grimsby House and Imogen's territory in the woods, and Josie didn't want to draw out either of those audiences to her work. Here was better too. There was a crossroads on the path not too far into the park from this entrance, which would be where Papa Legba was willing to meet them.

Bell parked the bike, and Josie unlatched herself from around his waist with a wistful reluctance. He was a broad man, and he had felt nice against her. She snorted, covering the sound with the scuff of her boots on the gravel. Not nice. *Sinful.*

"If you wanted to have a seance, we coulda gone to the graveyard," Bell said, leg swinging over the back of the bike as he stared at the entrance to the preserve.

"I told you. This is different." Josie helped herself to the storage compartment under the seat, pulling out her bag as it clanked with bottles and candles and the soft rattle of the tambourine.

"What kind of different?" Bell asked, falling into step with her as she headed for the path.

"You saw my altar?" Josie asked, amused as the giant, handsome demon at her side shifted uncomfortably as if he were feeling guilty. Was it terrible that she'd still found him handsome when he'd revealed himself and cornered her earlier? Maybe not handsome, but powerful for sure, and that was a kind of attraction too. "Do you know who it was for?"

Bell frowned and shrugged. "Some kind of... kitchen... spirit?"

She scoffed. "Okay, wow. Yeah, never mind. I'ma let you be surprised instead."

Kitchen spirit. Demons didn't know shit, apparently. Josie found that somewhat comforting, and her steps bounced as she pushed forward. It was cold, but she was wearing the sweater June had gifted her and Bell radiated heat, or at least the illusion of it.

"So. You're really all about this whole... corrupting good and spreading evil lifestyle, hm?"

Bell's shoulders drew in slightly around his ears, and his eyes tracked the woods around them as if he were expecting to be spied on. "It's in men's nature to fall, to be corrupted."

"So?" Josie asked. "Why force the issue?"

Bell blinked. "We were cast out of our home for a weaker creation."

Josie frowned up at him. "What's so great about being superior?" Bell frowned back at her but didn't answer. "So that's it? Your goal is to prove to...you know," she pointed upwards.

"The Maker."

"The Maker," she said, eyebrows raising. "You're trying to prove that humans weren't worth it?"

"It's more complicated than that."

"But what if *you're* wrong?" Josie asked. "What if a flaw is deserving of love too, and actually all y'all are just assholes?"

"And the murderer?" Bell replied. "They're just...what? A charming little error in the fabric of this town? Is homicide a flaw deserving of love?"

"Hmm. Okay, fair point. But you're not responsible for the murderer, so I'm not sure it helps your argument. Humans can prove themselves inferior without demons showing up. This way," she said, catching his elbow and turning right on the path, heading to the far side of the preserve, away from Sweet Pea.

"I don't want to go back," Bell said, voice weaving through the trees, spoken soft and private. "If that's what you're thinking. I'm not trying to be redeemed. We were created with flaws too, and mine was to not prefer paradise. I serve the one who gave me a home I deserved, and a purpose I excelled at."

"Well..." Josie mulled over the words. "I can't argue with that, I suppose. If following orders suits you."

"You're misunderstanding me intentionally."

"Maybe your case isn't that strong," she said, grinning at his glare. "Have you had this argument before?"

He turned away, facing ahead. So no, he had not. She stopped at the corner of the crossroads, a great oak tree growing at the spot, its roots churning under the ground and making the path uneven.

"Here," she said, kneeling in the grass.

Bell turned to study the area. "You're calling the Devil at midnight?"

"It's not midnight yet, and no, I'm not on any kind of terms with the Devil," Josie said, pulling supplies out of her bag. The bottle of rum, cork pulled out so the liquor spiced the air. She set the brownies on a black and red dish with a pipe filled with tobacco balanced on the edge. There was a corn husk doll painted in red and black, wearing a tiny straw hat. She lit a St. Peter candle, Papa Legba's saintly counterpoint, and sprinkled a handful of pennies around its base.

As offerings went, it met the requirements, even if it wasn't quite as plentiful as she might have wished. Especially considering this was Virginia, not New Orleans, and it was only her here. Her and Bell. She was hoping the demon might be a little bit of a draw for Legba. Josie grabbed the last two items in the bag, the tambourine from her altar and a black cloth she'd embroidered with Legba's vévé, or sigil, in red silk threads. Mémé had taught her the work as a little girl, and Josie had a drawer with every Loa's cloth and colors carefully pressed between clean cotton, for whenever she might need them.

"I've never seen that symbol before," Bell said, crouching down to her side. When his hand reached out to touch the red lines of leaves and curls, Josie swatted at his fingers and he pulled back.

"You just stand here and look pretty," she said, rising up.

Bell smirked and followed her, stepping back as she pushed her hands against his stomach to guide him behind her.

"You think I should be scared of your spirit, Cupcake?" Bell said, a laugh at the back of the words. "Doubt they could do me much harm, but it's sweet of you to care."

"Oh, I will laugh if he goes after you, don't you worry. It would serve you right," Josie answered. She shook the nervous tension out of her body, and the tambourine in her hand jangled and chimed. Bell's arms crossed over his chest, the movement rustling in the corner of her eye. It was hard not to be self-conscious with him looming behind her like a shadow, but she'd asked him here, and this next part had always been her favorite growing up.

She hummed a note, stomping her heel on the ground and knocking the tambourine against the heel of her palm. She couldn't remember the words right away, but she didn't need to be picky about the song. She bounced in place and found a beat and closed her eyes. Mémé had always liked the old hymns, leading the party through melody as other members picked up instruments. Josie missed the community after she and her mother had ridden out of state. Vodou wasn't the celebration she loved as a girl when she was by herself. The coven was closer, but nothing really compared.

The night was quiet, and Bell was silent behind her as Josie hummed and mumbled and danced in a small circle, tambourine cymbals crashing. The air was empty of any magic but her own and her rickety voice. She wasn't a good singer, and right now she wasn't even an enthusiastic singer. Papa Legba wouldn't come for this. She had to do better.

She took a deep breath and called out, "Papa Legba, come an' visit. Your lil' child is waitin'. Papa Legba, come and open the gates!"

She repeated the words, making up a melody, inventing a rhythm for a dance. Bell's eyes caught hers as they opened, but she ignored his puzzled expression, turning a grin up to the stars and rattling the tambourine over her head. Josie spun and spun in a circle, until her heart was hammering and the stars were spinning and laughter was breaking into her chant.

Then she heard the trumpets, faint and distant. Bell tensed, and Josie held her arm to block him as he stepped forward. She sang, trying to sweeten her call, thumping her instrument at her side. Piano keys jangled, a bass drummed sweetly, and horns circled the crossroads. Finally, a shadow strolled out from behind the oak.

"Well, well," Papa Legba crooned and croaked in greeting. He was a rickety old spirit, wearing a child's wide grin surrounded by black wrinkles. A bony chest swayed inside of too big overalls, arms flapping at his side as he took his comical stride forward. The grass crunched dry beneath his feet as he stepped, and everything cracked and snapped and groaned as he crouched down and lit the pipe on the St. Peter candle.

"Evening, Papa Legba," Josie said, lowering her chin to

her chest in greeting, a private thrill racing through her. He had come. And not even jumped into her skin, he had just *walked out*. This was an honor, and she couldn't even tell Mémé about it.

"You don' write. You don' call," Legba teased, and the pipe puffed smoke to hide his smile. Bell was vibrating at her side, and Legba's straw hat tipped as the spirit examined the demon. "Interestin' company you keepin', Piti bean."

Josie's heart swelled and ached hearing Mémé's name for her on Legba's twisted tongue. He was right. It had been a *long* time since she'd been in the presence of the Loa. It felt like coming home, and even better, he greeted her as such.

"Beleth, King of Hell," Josie said, gesturing to the demon. "Meet Papa Legba, gatekeeper of the spirit world."

Bell was stiff, and Legba was grinning, head tipped back but eyes invisible. Neither of them moved for a long stretch, and Josie wanted to kick Bell if he was about to get her in trouble with Legba. Bell twitched and then his head tipped in a brief bow, eyes never lowering from Legba's face.

Papa Legba snorted and puffed on the pipe. "Look at 'is head spinnin'. Ne'er seen nothin out 'is own lil' bubble, eh now?"

"And how many of my kind have met you?" Bell asked, voice near a whisper and edgy with tension.

"Oh, a fair few, I should say," Legba answered, sharp shoulders bobbing. "Now 'dere. Whatcha need from me, cher? Should I be callin' Ghede Linto? 'Cause I'll tell ya, he won't like yer friend here."

"No, Papa. I have questions for two mortal spirits who were killed in this wood last week," Josie said.

Cold trickled down Josie's spine as the smoke cleared between them, and Legba was no longer smiling. He stepped in closer and Josie kept rigid, waiting for his approach.

"Now cher, you know what's dead is best left dead. And I seen these spirits on my way. They in no fit shape to be visiting." His head tilted down, examining the offerings left between them, and Josie folded her lips between her teeth to keep from speaking while he thought over her request. "I will answer you one question on their behalf, on account a' your Mémé in good favor."

Josie's breath rushed out of her in one great relieved gust. She hoped this conversation didn't get back to Mémé, but she would brace herself for how to explain the situation if she had to. "I need to know who killed them, Papa Legba. Before the town starts lookin' at witches."

Bell's gaze was hard on her face, and she ignored his stare. What had he thought? That a small town wouldn't start to come up with its own conclusion to the mystery of a funky ritual site in the woods, and the murder of two strangers?

Legba hunkered down again, creaking like an old house, and gathered the pennies into gnarled fingers, clinking them with gentle tosses. He hummed, and the sound became a whine. Josie's heart sank as he rose again, head shaking slowly side to side. His hand reached out to her chest and Josie swallowed and nodded, shooting Bell a warning look before he could speak.

Legba's palm landed on her sternum and then...

—The tent rustled—again, for like the fiftieth freaking time —and she rolled into Jake's chest. Raccoons or whatever. Except then the sound wasn't a rustle at all, but a slice and tear and ripping. It was in her head as she slept, and waking took too long. There were knees digging into her back before she could even groan, and by the time she was ready to scream—

—Jake scrambled, a weak and cracking cry of refusal breaking out of his throat as Danielle gave a wet gurgle, thrashing limbs at his side. Shit. He was shit. Shit! He slid out of the tear in the tent, hot piss running down his thigh. His feet weren't awake, or he was too fucking terrified because he couldn't get his legs up underneath him. The attacker was on him, heavy and solid, with a fist in his hair. Jake was—

Josie gasped, and Bell's fingers dug into her shoulders, drawing her back with a yank to his chest. She slapped her hand over her mouth to stifle her scream and gasped through her fingers, sucking down breaths and trying to banish the feeling of a warm, sticky blade against her throat.

"They was scared. And then they was dead," Legba said.

Josie swallowed and nodded, ignoring the ache still lingering. She'd known before he showed her, knew it was a possibility, but it stung all the same. "I understand," she said, words a little raspy. "Thank you, Papa Legba."

The campers hadn't seen the killer.

Bell's grip tightened on her again, and then he released her. Legba's gaze strayed over her shoulder, and his lips twitched with a smirk. The question of Josie's mother burned in her chest but Legba had said 'one.' Asking another question would require a favor to the dead, and she wasn't certain she was prepared to pay, especially after being slammed with those memories.

Legba looked down at her, his stare just twin blazes of light underneath the deep shadow of the brim of his black straw hat. He grinned, and his skin creased and chipped like ash curling on a burning log.

"Would yous like to know a secret, ma cher?"

He offered it, which meant she was safe from any debt. Josie's fingers brushed over her throat, and she nodded. "If you would like to share it, Papa, I sure would."

He bent at the waist, like a lordly gentleman, even though he was barely an inch taller than her. Bony fingers wrapped around her own in a gentle touch, and his pipe smoke curled around her shoulders in an acrid embrace. A paper dry cheek rested against Josie's, and his voice in her ear was the scratch of bone on the silk lining of her own coffin.

"She all right, cher. Not good, not bad. Somebody put an itch in dat woman's feet, and she ain't never gon' stay still for you. But she all right."

Josie's eyes drifted shut. She nodded and sighed. "Thank you, Papa."

A cold kiss drifted over her cheek. "Sing me out, Piti bean."

Josie nodded, and Bell slipped the tambourine back into her hand with a warm grip of his fingers around hers. She must have dropped it during the memory gift. With Papa Legba present, some of the words came back to her, the Creole songs Mémé loved to dance to. She found a sweeter, slower, funeral march rhythm, and Legba nodded in approval, packing the offerings she'd brought into a sack on his shoulder, leaving only the plate and candle and her carefully stitched vévé behind. He strolled out to her music, and Josie's voice choked on the notes as salty tears squeezed their way out of the corners of her eyes, despite her efforts to hold them back.

When the music was hollow, she gave a last rattle of the tambourine and fell still. All the energy washed right out of her with the ritual ended and Legba gone. Shit, she was *exhausted*. It was a shame she hadn't brought extra brownies, 'cause she could really use one right about now. She swayed in step and Bell caught her by the shoulder, his fingertips on her sweater. Josie blushed at the reminder of her witness.

She hadn't forgotten that he was there, more like she'd forgotten who he really was. She rolled her cheeks against her shoulders to wipe away the tears, and then turned to face him.

"Well, it was worth a shot," she said, shrugging up at the demon. Bell's eyes were wide, and brow furrowed, his hands hovering around her arms like he was waiting for her to faint. She realized he hadn't said a word since Legba had dismissed him. "You okay?"

With that, Bell scoffed, hands dropping to his side as he spun away. "Let's just get back."

15 CONFUSED IS A FOUR-LETTER WORD

Bell was not okay. His head was spinning with revelations he'd never been particularly interested in, and *worse*, he found himself keenly aware of the way Josie seemed about two steps from falling asleep or swooning. Even her color was off, paler than it should've been with the faint dusting of freckles on her nose standing out too vividly. He was...

No. Not going there.

If he had to deal with one confusing concept, let it be the spirit he'd just met.

"You never heard of Vodou before?" Josie asked as she finished packing up her bag.

Bell jammed his hands in his pockets as they started to walk. "Heard of it." But he'd thought it was one of those things humans made up and played with when they wanted to rebel or feel dangerous, play at their own demonic impulses. He hadn't really understood.

He certainly hadn't been fucking prepared to meet Legba—he refused to call the spirit *Papa*. Legba was an anomaly. Not a whiff of demon on him, but not the glowing saint he would've expected a witch like Josie to call on. The being was shadowy, and so *heavy* it made Bell's skull hurt. It was like walking into a room with Morningstar glaring at him. Whatever or whoever Legba was, if he *had* been a demon, he would've outranked Bell by a startling distance.

He didn't like that. He didn't like the way Legba had swamped Josie with the memories of the murdered humans either. She kept touching her throat like she was feeling for a scar.

Angels, demons, men, and the Maker. That was the structure of the world Bell existed in, and now that structure was cracked open and new universes were falling in. He'd only had a taste. Worse, Legba had said Bell wasn't the first demon he'd met, which meant that *others* knew and hadn't fucking said anything, and that made him feel like a damn idiot.

"It's not totally unrelated, you know," Josie said.

Bell grunted, glancing down at her. "What do you mean?"

"Vodou, the Loa—like Legba—they align with saints in Catholicism. Rosa, she's familiar with the Orisha, and those are more mirrors of the Loa and the saints. There's overlap," Josie said. Which was all more than Bell was completely prepared to swallow in this moment. Her smile hitched. "Not to say I didn't kind of freak out when I learned demons were real. I thought maybe I needed to call up Mémé and talk about converting."

"Who?" Legba had said that name too.

"My grandmother. She's a Vodou priestess. Makes regular calls to Papa Legba, although our family does more work with the Ghedes and... and this is all kind of a lot for you right now, isn't it?"

He wanted to say no, that he could fucking handle whatever she had to throw at him. But if that included more introductions to beings like Legba, then that would've been a lie.

"A bit, yeah," he said, and tried not to enjoy the beaming, humored smile she shared with him. "You're from—"

"New Orleans. N'awlins," she said, slurring the two words into one curling sound, heavy with affection. "But my mom moved us out when I was a kid, and I've only been back for visits a couple times since I graduated high school. Never had the money for the trip when I was studying, and then I had the business—which I can never fucking get away from."

Bell stared at her as the words spun out. She was so... open. Like they were... like he was just a human too, and she could talk to him the way she did with anyone else. Was he also supposed to share stories now? Did he tell her about the time he'd raised an army of dead in the lowlands outside of Damascus?

"Normally they possess us," Josie said, grabbing his attention back. She shifted her bag on her shoulder again like it was twice as heavy as before, and he remembered that she was tired. "The Loa. We call them and they ride us, communicate and work that way. I've never seen one appear that way before. I suppose he didn't fancy you for his vessel."

Bell stiffened. "Is that why you brought me?"

Josie's smile was sly. "No. I thought he'd think you were amusing. Worth the trip."

And she was right. And Bell found he wasn't even mad. "Your coven is something different though," Bell said.

Josie nodded, and her eyelids were heavy. He would have to keep an eye on her as they rode back to Sweet Pea.

"June is..." she paused, and her gaze slid sideways to him, narrowed in study.

"What?"

"I'm trying to decide if this is information I shouldn't be sharing."

Truth be told, Bell had forgotten about the line that was supposed to be separating them. It was getting foggy in his head.

Josie shrugged and continued. "June is kind of in charge. Not totally but she and Imogen come from a long line of occultism and witchcraft, and I dunno even know what else. They've got an arsenal of information in their heads. And their style works for me. I don't really wanna share the little I learned from Mémé with them, if it's going to be adapted and diluted."

She had shared it with him. Bell decided not to point that out.

"Anyway, it's different up here. Like the Loa aren't as present. I pay my respects because I *do* respect them, but there's other energy in this—" Her speech broke off suddenly, and she stilled, eyes growing huge. "Do you hear that?" she whispered, barely audible.

Bell froze, waiting in the silence, the woods holding its breath with them. He scanned the darkness, hunting for a shadow, and Josie's shoulders were just starting to relax when they heard the sound. A twig cracked underfoot, echoing in the quiet, and Bell caught sight of a hooded figure stepping out from behind a tree. His hand reached out to grab Josie and caught on air as she took off like a rocket toward the sound, her bag dropped to the ground.

"Don't be stupid," Bell called after her.

It was wasted breath *and* time. The figure took off in a

zig-zagging line through the trees, and there was enough light from the moon overhead for Josie to follow.

"Hey! Hey stop, asshole!" Josie cried.

"Josie!" Bell barked, and then he realized that he *was* an idiot, but so was she, and she was going to chase that person through the dark. And it wasn't lost on him that someone running through the woods and refusing to answer when called was probably the murderer.

His feet were planted in the ground, body coiled tighter than a spring. This wasn't his problem. *Josie* wasn't his problem. Never mind that he shouldn't have come out here tonight with her, what compelling reason was there for him to wait for her? To worry about her?

The crashing chaos of the two running through the woods grew fainter, and Bell tried to force himself to turn and find his way back to the bike. He could wait for Josie there or— No. He could just *leave*.

Neither of those things happened when a sudden and short scream snapped through the air, before being immediately cut off. Bell was off the path before the silence returned, legs bending and warping into an animal lean for better speed. He damned himself for letting them get a head start, for trying to fool himself that he wouldn't chase after her. Trees whipped past him as he raced, hearing heightened with growing ears, growl rising in his throat at the sound of bodies scuffling on the ground.

His blood scorched through his veins as he hunted them down. *If she was hurt...* His gnarled feet stumbled over the thought. She was *human*. She was a witch.

And then he saw them up ahead, tangled in briars. Josie was trying to claw herself up off the ground, but the attacker was on her back, hands around her throat, and she was barely managing to squeak, let alone breathe. What Josie was or was not ceased to matter.

Bell roared, and the attacker scrambled off Josie, a foot kicking her in the ribs on their way up. Bell braced to leap, to tackle the fucker to the ground and *rip* their throat out, until he saw Josie sagging on the ground. She wasn't catching her breath, her hands still scrambling on the ground in front of her as she fought for air. Something was bruised or broken, and there wasn't enough time to catch the killer. Bell skidded to her side, flipping her on to her back. Josie whimpered, eyes wide with terror and tried to scuttle backwards into a briar, until Bell caught her by her shoulder.

He drew his human shape back up and she settled, chest heaving and body shaking as he laid his palm gently over the top of her throat. It'd been a long time since he'd done any healing, and for a moment he wondered if he'd lost the skill in the Fall from Grace. Then warmth gathered on his palm, a ticklish feeling, and there was an audible pop. Josie sobbed and then gasped, arching as he steadied her. He turned and stared through the dark—searching for the attacker, ready to continue the chase—when a small hand wrapped around his wrist. Josie was collapsed in the under-growth, breaths unsteady but deep, eyes blinking slowly up at the tops of the trees before drifting slowly in his direction.

She was clinging to him, her hands covering his, and the weight of the touch pinned him in place. "You'll be fine," he said, too abrupt.

She nodded and winced as she swallowed, breath rattling. "What was it?" Bell frowned at the question, and she asked again, "What kind of spirit was it? Demon?"

Oh. He lifted his head and closed his eyes, trying to feel

for anything unusual, but instead he found adrenaline and sweat and stress.

"Human," he said.

Josie hummed and released his hands for a moment, and he suffered brief confusion about what to do with his own body in the moment, and then she was gripping his arms and pulling herself upright. Bell sat back on his heels when she was close enough to smell, the vanilla and fear mingling together into something unexpectedly unpleasant.

"Are they gone?" He nodded to answer her, wondering if he should do something about the scratch in her voice. "Home then," she said, eyes tracing skittishly through the dark.

He lifted her up by her elbows, tried not to be too obvious as he brushed her clean, finding snags in the sweater she wore.

"Shit," she whispered, spotting one on her sleeve. "June is gonna kill me."

Bell snorted. Considering the act of killing Josie had almost taken place tonight without June's interference, he wasn't sure if that should be her main concern. "Ash can fix it," he said instead, and then they both blinked at each other.

Ashtaroth would not be fixing her sweater, because Bell would sure as fuck not be telling any of the others about anything that had happened tonight. And if Josie asked Ash herself, Bell would probably set him on fire.

"Come on." He pressed his hand to her back and urged her forward, back the way he'd come on a more direct route to the path. With every tripping step and anxious shiver that ran down her back, Bell found himself resisting the urge to scoop Josie up to his chest and sprint his way back to the motorcycle. Was it justified if it meant he would have her home and away from him sooner?

"I didn't know you could heal," Josie said, voice whispering.

Bell snorted. "How much do you really know about what demons *are* capable of?"

She hummed. "I think I read something about... 'unspeakable evils?'"

He tried to hide his laugh, but her smile was glinting up at him out of the corner of his eye, so he must have failed. "We have the gifts of angels, put to wrong purpose."

She was quiet, and Bell released a silent sigh. Just get back to the bike, ride to Sweet Pea, leave her at the door, and try never to wonder any of the eighteen million flitting thoughts in his head ever again.

"Always wrong purpose?" Josie asked.

His heart clenched like a fist in his chest, and that was the last straw. Bell spun and bent, let his eyes glow with warning sparks, as he shoved his face into her view. What did it mean that he enjoyed the whiff of her fear when it was *his* actions that caused it, but not others'?

"If you're wondering if my position in Hell is a clerical error, *no*," he growled, words grinding in his throat. "I earned my place, my rank."

Josie shuddered, eyes wide and lips parted, and Bell shoved down the lick of hunger in his stomach at her expression.

"So it's a kind of average?"

He blinked at her. Josie's lips twitched.

This would be easier if I thought she was insane, he thought. *Or stupid.*

"Alright," she said with a sigh, turning and stumbling forward again, until Bell rushed to catch up with her before she tripped over a branch. "You're evil, you're rotten, you're Mr. Bad News."

Bell grinned at the nickname. Maybe he could make that catch on in the Bowels when this was all over. "You're delirious. Did they hit you over the head?"

"Don't think so," Josie mumbled, reaching up and running her hand over her bare head. His hand reached out to follow the same path. He admitted only to himself that it was just so he knew what it felt like, the soft prickles of her hair on his human skin. When she leaned into the touch just a fraction, he dropped his hand back to his side.

Josie picked her bag up off the ground when they reached the path, and they walked the rest of the way in silence. When they made it to the bike, Bell fought a brief battle with himself until he saw Josie's eyes drooping shut. He perched on the back of his seat, arms plenty long enough to reach the handles.

"Here," he said, patting his lap. Josie's eyebrows rose on her forehead, and he schooled his expression into stern neutrality. "I didn't save your life just to let you go skidding across the pavement when you fall off my bike half-asleep. Sit here."

She was so small anyway, what difference did it make? Bell reached out and tugged at her waist, hefting her onto the seat in front of him, facing him with her legs around his waist. She sat stiffly, eyes wide with surprise, forehead just in front of his lips.

"I need to be able to catch you if I have to," he muttered, and then ended the discussion by kicking the engine to life with a roar.

Josie's arms curled around his back and up his shoulders, under the cover of his leather jacket, as Bell walked his bike into motion and gave it gas. Her head was tucked beneath his chin as he rode, fingers clutching over his shoulder blades. If he still had them, she would've been touching his wings, and the thought gave him a jolt of discomfort. He'd meant to be practical, and as Josie softened against him—her breasts against his chest and warm breath on his pulse—he realized he'd landed on intimate instead. And he was fairly sure he couldn't blame his satisfaction at the way she fit against him on a human hunger. This was pride and vanity and lust all churning together in him.

It took longer to reach Sweet Pea than he would've liked, and also somehow not nearly long enough. By the time he was pulling his bike into the alley behind Josie's shop, he suspected she might have been dozing.

Carry her inside, a wicked voice suggested, and he thought of sliding back the sheets on Josie's bed, taking her shoes off and tucking her in. There was a version where she parted those heavy lashes of hers, and he slid in beside her too.

Fuck no.

"Wake up," he grunted, and she jerked back, head knocking against his chin.

"Ah! Ow. Huh?" She blinked as Bell unwound her limbs from around him and stood. "Oh. Okay."

She was sleepy and soft, and she practically fell off the seat of his bike. Bell thought he might be grinding his teeth down to smooth stubs the longer he was around her. Her voice was croaking, and she fumbled in her jeans pocket for her keys, steps plodding to her door. Bell dug her bag out from the compartment in his bike and crossed to her, setting it on her shoulders.

"Thanks," she rasped.

By the light over her door, he could see the shadows growing on her throat, anger boiling in his gut.

"Look up at me," he ordered.

Josie turned her head and tilted it back to look up at him. There was no reserve in her gaze, no fear, no teasing.

You've already lost the battle, he thought, but he wasn't sure which of them he meant. His hands reached up, and Josie didn't even flinch as he cupped his fingers over the growing bruises. Warmth spread through his touch into her skin, ready and willing this time, and Josie sighed, her eyes drifting shut in relief. When she opened them again, there was something in their dark depths that Bell recognized as inherently dangerous to his well being. And in spite of that, he might have considered standing there and soaking it in for another hour or week at least.

"Goodnight, Mr. Bad News," Josie said, cheeks swelling with her smile.

"Goodnight, Cupcake," Bell said, head tilting down to hers before he caught himself and turned away.

His haste in pulling away on his bike was born out of self-preservation more than impatience to leave.

CHAD SCHMIDT, property developer, was jacking off to mediocre porn when all the electricity in his hotel room cut out at once.

"Shit," he hissed. "Shit, shiiiit."

Despite the fact that his laptop wasn't plugged in but was now dead—as well as every single tiny LED light in the room—Chad was too deeply embedded in the fantasy to quit working his dick *now*. He was fucking close, and even though he claimed to hate the entire concept of imagination, he could still hear the high pitched siren squeak of the woman he'd been focusing on for the past three minutes.

"So close," he said, as a personal congratulatory mantra. "So close!"

"Does your hand cramp around a dick that small?" a deep voice asked in the dark.

Later, when the shock of what came next had lessened, Chad would wonder to himself if it was the low tenor of the man's voice that sent him writhing and groaning, cum splattering over his stomach, or just the element of surprise.

"Ahhhhfuuuckkkyaaaaa," Chad shouted, even as he scrambled back against the headboard.

"Fucking humans," the voice muttered.

Chad was catching his breath, wondering why that was one of the best orgasms he could recall, when his sheets set on fire and the figure at the foot of the bed was illuminated by the glow. He screamed, kicking down the sheet, his boxers tangled around his thighs, and stared at the handsome man in front of him with vivid coal red eyes.

"What the fuck? What the fuck? Who the fuck are you?!"

Bell watched as the man tried to climb his way out of his burning bed. He raised his hands, and Chad's bedsheets wrapped themselves like snakes around his wrists, dragging his arms out to the corners of the mattress. Chad's screams escalated, steady brief exclamations of terror, not unlike the porn star's repetitive shouts of feigned ecstasy. Bell waited for the noise to settle, his nose wrinkling as pungent urine soaked the bed.

"Please. Please, let me go," Chad whimpered, drawing his legs back to try and avoid the flames, failing to realize that if they hadn't already burnt him they weren't going to.

The illusion was thorough, right down to the smoke billowing up and the curling red lace of fire on cotton, but Bell didn't want any unnecessary visitors, so he wasn't *actually* setting the bed on fire. Chad was an idiot.

"I need you to listen to me and quit staining the linens, Chad Schmidt," Bell murmured, circling the edge of the bed to tower over the quivering human. "I don't care what you do in this town. I don't care what you turn that preserve into when you get your hands on it. I have one rule for you. If you break it again, I will cut you open with a nail clipper and hang your innards around this hotel room like fucking party streamers."

There was a soft whistle of air and the stench of shit.

"For fuck's sake," Bell breathed, covering his eyes.

"Man, I don't know what you're talking about. I- I- Oh, Jesus! No!"

Chad screeched as Bell transformed into his beast, finally free and whole in his form again, claws popping through the cover of the mattress as he pinned the man down, snarling muzzle snapping over the thin flesh of a tender throat.

"The girl is off limits!" Bell growled. "You lay another finger on her, and you're dead. And when you're dead, I can guarantee that you will be seeing me again, because I know exactly where you're going next!"

Chad Schmidt sobbed, snot bubbling in his nostrils, and head tossing. "What girl? What girl? I didn't- I didn't! Not since college."

Bell's eyes narrowed on the man's red and sweating face. Below, Chad's cock stirred and lifted hopefully upwards. It was a natural reaction to fear that would haunt the man with confusion for a long time to come. Bell huffed and jumped off the bed, digging through the human's thoughts. Chad Schmidt had spent the evening in the hotel bar, attempting to find a sexual partner and striking out unanimously. He had definitely not been in the woods, and had just completed masturbating for the second time that night.

The girl he mentioned was a drunk and reluctant one night stand from decades ago who had been resentfully persuaded to sleep with him. Whenever an inkling of remorse stirred up over the experience, Chad helpfully reminded himself that she'd said yes eventually.

"I see," Bell said. He felt no particular inklings of remorse for being perhaps a little too hasty in assuming this man was the killer. After all, nothing was actually on fire, and Chad Schmidt was a weevil of a human being.

Bell sighed and rolled his shoulders, drawing up his human disguise again. He flicked his fingers, dulling the details of the conversation in Chad's mind, but leaving the general impression. At the very least, he'd ensured the man wouldn't have an appetite for pastry any time soon.

"Wait!" Chad cried as Bell moved to the door. The room still glowed orange with a fire that never grew. "Wait! You gotta let me go! Please! Please!"

The door shut behind Bell with a soft click, the neon lighting of the hall flicking on again. Inside the hotel room, the high pitched moans of the woman on the computer started up again, and Chad whimpered as he watched the screen, entirely uncertain what to do about his latest erection.

16 BAD ALIBIS

The next day, Josie cursed herself for not considering *why* the killer might have been in the woods in the first place. She was exhausted from calling Papa Legba, confused from the extended time spent with Bell, and then just relieved not to be dead. If she had two more brain cells to rub together, she might have deduced what happened.

Instead, June entered the bakery through the back door in the early hours before either of their shops were open, her hands wringing in front of her. "There's been another murder on the preserve," she said.

Josie paused in her mixing of the choux pastry for just a beat, before picking up again and pushing her worry down through her arms and into the motion.

"Last night. This one has a circle too."

"Shit," Josie said, eyes closing. Pastry splattered over the edge of the pan, burning the back of her hand. "Shit. June, what do we do?" She opened her mouth to tell June about Bell and Legba, about the killer in the woods, about being strangled.

But none of it had come to anything. She had no

answers from Legba, only the horrific memory of the campers' deaths, and no bruises around her neck after Bell had taken care of her.

Bell...

Not the time, she scolded herself, and locked away the memory of his hands on her skin or the heat of him as she curled around his chest on the way home.

"We answer all the questions we're asked. When they want to know where we were last night, we tell them. Alibis or not."

"Fuck!" Josie shouted, and slammed the pan on the burner.

The choux pastry was split, and she was completely screwed. June stood frozen, just out of the corner of her eye, and Josie turned the stove off and faced her.

"I was in the woods last night," Josie said, watching June. "With Beleth," she added reluctantly. That got a response, just a faint one because June was a queen at keeping her shit under control, but Josie caught the slight widening of her gray eyes.

She spilled the story from beginning to end, skipping over the ride home and that half-second of excitement where she thought the demon was about to kiss her goodnight.

"I see..." June said, squaring her shoulders and taking in a deep breath as she absorbed the information.

"If you were an investigator, you'd think that was some crazy bullshit," Josie said, scrubbing her hand over her head.

"As a story it... probably needs to be simplified," June agreed. "I'd say you could say you were at my place but I was at Imogen's and—"

"And I'm sure someone in this nosy ass town saw me on the back of that bike heading out of town," Josie agreed.

"So you went to the preserve at night with an attractive new man in town," June said, all matter of fact.

"A preserve where a couple was recently murdered," Josie pointed out, eyebrows raised. She turned back to her stove, scraped out the failed dough, and set herself to start over. "At a scene where they found two sets of footprints?"

"Maybe you're... into that sort of thing? The macabre?" June suggested. "It's better than being caught in a lie. Better than being the killer, too."

"Not as good as if I'd just kept my dumb ideas to myself and stayed home," Josie said, plopping butter into the warm pan with a sigh.

"Yes, well... next time," June said. "It's a shame you have to give the demon an alibi though."

Josie frowned and glanced at June over her shoulder. "But we know it wasn't them."

June shrugged. "We also know they're here to do potentially worse."

Josie swallowed, whipping flour into the butter in her pan. The night before she'd been so grateful when Bell had healed the bruises off her neck. It solved the problem of what to explain to others, not to mention the radiating burn and ache in her throat. She'd admit, only to herself, that she'd taken the gesture as a kind of truce between them. How bad could a demon really be when they were capable of kindness of that measure? Now, perhaps it would've been better if the bruises were still there, and she could say they'd tried to catch the killer. Maybe it would clear their own names.

"Right. So. Just say I was in the woods, with Bell. Hope he doesn't blow my alibi. Hope the investigators don't automatically assume *we're* the murderers. Doesn't sound stressful at all. Who was it, by the way?" Josie asked. "Who was killed?"

"The Ranger. Imogen said it looked like maybe he'd surprised the killer, because the circle wasn't complete."

"Imogen saw it?"

"She found it."

That's twice now, Josie thought. Once was a coincidence. Twice was...

The timer went off behind her, and Josie took a deep breath. "Can you grab an oven mitt and check the canelés?"

Twice was probably Imogen keeping an eye on the woods. Josie really didn't need to start side-eyeing her friends. And it definitely wasn't Imogen who'd been digging their knee into her back last night. Imogen was tall but she wasn't heavy like that.

"I spent the night at Imogen's, Josie," June said softly.

Shit. "I know, babe," Josie said, nodding too fast. "I know."

She needed to get it together, especially before the investigators showed up.

AT FIRST, it was nice to have a slow day in the bakery. Her head was buzzing like a beehive with worries and she'd had to start half her recipes over again throughout the morning. But by noon, with only a small handful of tourists stopping by, Josie realized what was happening. How long had it taken, she wondered, before the word of the latest murder scene spread, and the locals started looking at her? At Rosa, June, and Imogen? It was the twenty-first century, and they hadn't made a secret of their practices. For the most part, the population of Sweet Pea was charmed by their local coven rather than wary, but these murders were bad press. They'd be worse than that if the real murderer wasn't caught.

She was about to text Rosa to see if business was slow, or she'd gotten a weird vibe from anyone, when the shop bells rang and and in walked the investigators.

"Detective Bagley. Sergeant Crowley," she said, a strange combination of anxiety and relief bubbling up in her, and reminding her that she'd had nothing to eat but pastry fumes yet that day.

"Miss Benoit. We'd like to ask you a couple questions about last night."

"Of course," Josie nodded and gestured to her tables. "Why don't y'all have a seat and I'll bring some coffee and extras up."

"We'd also like your permission to search your apartment, but at this point it's entirely voluntary."

At this point, Josie thought, pressing her hand to her stomach where it flipped and tossed.

"I'm happy to hand the keys over to your team," Josie said, eyeing the officers waiting on the sidewalk outside. "Door's round back. Sticks a little when you turn it."

"We appreciate your cooperation," Crowley said, eyes narrowing to the contrary.

"Trust me, Sergeant. I've got no interest in being the squeaky wheel."

She just wished she had a lawyer she could call. Cornell was out because he'd be working for the county on this one. She'd ask him for a reference after the officers left. Damn her for not thinking of it before they'd arrived. Instead, she'd been holding her breath like an idiot, hoping somehow they'd all just forget about her.

When she returned with her keys and a tray of coffee

and food, Josie sat down at the table, handing over her keys to Mark Nolan. He didn't smile at her today. Barely even met her eyes.

Five years sucking up to everyone in Sweet Pea, building her shop's respect and reputation amongst an audience that still would've rather she made cupcakes. And now she was just gonna be the Murder Suspect around town. Outside, across the street, Mrs. Montgomery and her ladies who lunched stood outside Love & Lattes watching the activity of the Sheriff's department around the bakery, their hands raised over their mouths to hide the breakneck pace of their whispering.

"Now someone mentioned seeing you last night, heading out of town with..." Crowley frowned at his notes where Bell's name was missing. "On the back of the motorcycle."

"Yeah." Josie sighed, and raised her eyes to Detective Bagley, because of the two, he at least looked smarter. And a little less mean. "I took my stupid ass out to the preserve last night. On a date with...Bell," she said. Damnit, the demon didn't even have a last name. She blushed as Bagley's eyebrows raised. "I dunno his last name. He's down at the corner with the new motorcycle club."

"What were the pair of you doing at the preserve, Miss Benoit?" Bagley asked.

Josie sucked her teeth. "Well it was a date, so I guess you could call it sight-seeing," she said, offering a smile.

"We're gonna need better specifics than that," Crowley muttered. "If you'd prefer a formal setting, we can do the interview at the station. There won't be snacks," he said, eyeing her food with derision, "But it might help you take this seriously."

Josie sat up straight. Rude. But fair e-fucking-nough.

"We rode to the north entrance of the park." She rattled off their path, trying to remember what forks they'd taken. "Had normal conversation about our backgrounds. Stopped at the oak at the fork there. I think we were there for about a half hour. Fooling around," she said when Crowley shot her a look.

"Did you hear or see anything unusual while you were out?" Bagley asked.

"I thought I heard someone as we walked back, but it was dark, and neither of us saw anything," Josie said, the lie forming easily on her tongue. It was the closest she could get to saying there was someone else out there. "And truth be told, it's easy enough to convince yourself that a sound in the woods is just a critter."

"And the site of a recent murder seemed like a romantic place to have a walk, did it?" Crowley asked.

"It seemed like a private place," Josie answered. "And we were well away from that spot. S'pose it was a little bit of a thrill."

She pursed her lips and blushed as the men exchanged a brief roll of the eyes. Let them think what they want about her romantic habits, she decided. As long as they didn't think she was a killer.

***

JOSIE WAS LOOKING FORWARD to getting back to her apartment after a long day of bad news and worry and feeling like a bug under a microscope. Until she opened her apartment door and felt the disturbed rattle of the air after the place had been rifled through by officers. The living room looked untidy, but her bedroom was horribly worse.

Her phone rang in her pocket, and Josie answered

without looking, her eyes fixed to the clanging energy around her altar, everything rearranged and violated.

"Hey," she said, voice cracking with the tears rising up in her throat.

"Aw, babe," Rosa cooed. "Okay, I'm locking up and on my way."

"Kay," Josie managed to squeeze out.

She set the phone on the floor, and let Rosa hang up as one by one, she took each piece of her altar off the table, smoothing her fingers over the surface of dolls and talismans and bottles, like she could erase the touch of strangers.

"I'm sorry, you guys," she whispered, organizing each item in front of her, taking the altar cloth off and shaking it loose. She cleaned the altar at least every other week, but this would take a special kind of work. Some good cleansing and a lot of apologetic offerings.

"Oh my god, look at what they did to your closet!"

Josie turned, swiped tears off her cheeks with her hands, and found Rosa running to the disarray of her tiny closet. Shoes were spilling out of the space, all jumbled together in odd matches.

"I didn't know you had heels!" Rosa cried, spinning to face Josie on the floor. Her jaw dropped as she spotted the altar. "Ohhh, *honey*."

"They had a couple shoe prints from the first scene. They must've been looking for a match," Josie said, frowning at her shoes.

"Well you wear a six, so I seriously doubt they found what they were looking for. You have some dainty feet. Uh oh. Your vibrator's out on the bed."

"Oh for fuck's sake!" Josie moaned, covering her face with her hands.

She'd really needed that vibrator last night after being all snuggled up with Bell, and having him give her those bewildered bedroom eyes at her door. Now Mark Nolan and who the hell else had seen it as they rifled through her sheets.

"Come on," Rosa said, crossing to join her on the floor. "Let's tidy things up for the spirits, pour 'em a glass for the night. And then go get yourself one, alright?"

"You want to take me out in public?" Josie asked, frowning. "I'm like a social pariah now."

"Everyone at Gunney's is a social pariah, babe," Rosa said with a shrug. "It's not a clean place. And whatever to them, you know? We go. We smile. We drink. We have an alibi in case anyone else gets bludgeoned to death tonight."

Josie gasped. "Is that what happened?"

Rosa's red lips pursed, and she nodded. "So I hear. I was wondering if we're at serial killer yet, but apparently not because of circumstances. One more though, and the FBI will be in."

"This is too much," Josie whispered, head shaking slowly.

Rosa nodded. "I agree. So let's go drink."

17

VINES OF DISCORD

Gunney's was buzzing as Bell walked in with his crew behind him. Minus Danny, who wasn't of legal drinking age, and who'd said, 'No way, man. You guys are scary, but not half as scary as my sister'd be if she found out.' They really needed to find some more recruits. Ones who weren't scared of their sisters.

"Heard you were ordering in some kegs for your place," Chrissie greeted, arms crossed under her breasts as if she was hoping they caught Bell's eye.

"Not your selection," Bell said, eyeing the Lite drafts and basic beers.

"Oh, don't take me the wrong way," Chrissie said, voice growing sour as if she fully intended on him feeling her offense. "What do I care if you lighten my load around here?"

If the Inferno took off and Gunney's shut down, she would care.

"I'll have a lager," Bell said, watching Chrissie tense, wondering if she would refuse to serve him. But she eyed the bill in his hand and tossed her limp ponytail, going to fill his glass.

The Inferno might even kill two local birds with one stone if they were smart, and take out the restaurant High Top. It was all part of the plan. It was why he was here. So what was with this urge to try and tease Chrissie, and get her back on his good side?

You're a demon. You don't have a good side, he reminded himself. And it worked for a few minutes, until the door of the bar opened and the conversations in the room trickled off into quiet.

Josie was walking in with the pretty green witch Rosa, and Bell's teeth gritted as Josie's stare drifted right over him as if she didn't even see him. *It's her fault.* Then she passed under a lamp, and he saw that her eyes were puffy and red with recent tears, and he nearly broke the glass Chrissie handed him. He tracked the witches' movements to a small booth, watched Rosa press Josie into a seat before heading back to the bar to order their drinks. His men were lined up at the bar ordering so her friend would have a wait, and Josie was looking...*wrong*. Her shoulders were drawn in, her eyes were cast down, and he'd never seen her looking as if she felt out of place. And there was no lie he could tell himself that convinced him to enjoy her discomfort.

He slid into the seat across from Josie, and she took one brief glance at his hands wrapped around his beer before her stare went back to the edge of the table.

"Is your throat bothering you?" he asked when she didn't speak.

"Nope. All healed," she said, the attempt at brightness in her voice failing entirely. "Detectives came around to the shop today. You heard about the..."

He had. He practically smelled it when he'd woke up that morning. "They questioned *you*?"

He liked that she had spirit, but she sure as hell didn't look like a killer. Maybe a town this good was a little confused on that front.

"The fact that they keep finding these phony ritual sites has them looking at all of us," she said, glancing up at the bar to check on Rosa. "If the only people saying the rituals look fake, are the only people you know who practice the stuff, well..."

"You tell them about the—?" he gestured around his own neck.

Josie shook her head and lifted her chin. "You mean this perfectly normal and unstrangled neck?"

"Ah."

"Yeah. But I told them I was out there with you." His eyebrows raised, and she shrugged. "Someone would've seen us on the bike. Someone could've driven past it parked there too. I dunno, I got the lies all muddled in with the truth. They'll talk to you soon, I'm sure."

"Fine. We went to the preserve together," he said.

She looked at him then, finally and fully, and Bell tried to suppress his satisfaction, tried to find a reason to hold her gaze or the will to break it. Instead, he just sat there. Like a fuckin' idiot. Looking back at her.

"Okay," she said, lips lifting.

"Are we having a party?" Vinny purred, sliding up to the booth, his eyes fixed on Josie who glared back at him.

With one twitch of Vinny's foot towards the seat next to Josie, Bell was snarling. "Move your ass to the other end of the bar and find something useful to do."

"Why don't I help you with whatever you're working on right here?" Vinny asked, teeth bared behind his beard.

"Why don't you both head off so my friend can have her seat?" Josie asked, spine straight.

Bell willed her to look at him, and then wished he could throw his damn brain into a blender to see if it got her out of his system. Vinny's eyes were watching him, and Bell tipped his head in Josie's direction, sliding out of the booth just in time for Rosa's return. Pie was following the curly haired green witch, drink in hand, and a puzzle in his eyes as he looked between Vinny, Bell, and Josie.

"C'mon," Bell grunted to his men.

Dante had found another table of girls. Ash was chatting up a group of men that looked like they might be viable candidates for the crew. Aim and Barbie were missing, but at this point Bell was relieved. Maybe they would turn up with something productive, but at least they weren't underfoot when he was in a pissy mood.

"Don't be prickly, boss," Vinny hissed in his ear as they walked away. "I could help you work that angle if you're so interested."

"If the best you can do for the team is get in my way, you better rethink your goals, Vine," Bell answered.

Vinny snarled at him, hackles raising like a wolf, and stalked off to Dante's table.

"If you're going to put him in his place, at least do it thoroughly," Pie murmured. "You're just pissing him off this way."

"He's pissing *me* off," Bell answered, frowning at the hint of a whine in his voice.

"Then take him by the scruff with your teeth and set the order of the pack back in place," Pie said, raising his eyebrows and taking a sip of his drink.

Bell's head turned to look over his shoulder on an unconscious impulse, the heel of Josie's black sneakers peeking out from the edge of her booth. Pie was right. It was time to focus on the job.

THE SOUND of motorcycle engines pulling up in front of Inferno was a promising start to the next morning. They had their final inspection for a retail beer license that afternoon, and Bell found himself growing restless to begin the real work. When they'd arrived in Sweet Pea, he'd looked forward to the slow and methodical year of tackling the town's innocence. Now, he wondered if Hell's Bells shouldn't expedite the job and find their way back to the Bowels sooner rather than later.

"Recruits?" he asked, wandering out from the back of the bar where they had designated a booth for exclusive crew use.

Ashtaroth stood at the front windows, arms crossed over his chest, lips curling behind his beard. "Not sure they're what you were hoping for, boss."

Bell frowned. He'd thought maybe Aim and Barbie had found a few new members at Gunney's the night before, but the local dive had an element of loyalty he hadn't predicted. Now that the Inferno was finding its way, the first spark of resentment had caught on in the town. He joined Ash at the window as Cornell and Thurman, their effusive neighbors, unsaddled themselves from the back of a pair of cruising Honda motorcycles. Before they reached the door, a wide, dark sedan pulled to the curb and Bell's eyes narrowed at the men seated inside.

"The detectives," Ash said.

"I expected to hear from them," Bell said. Because Josie had warned him. And where would it be better to speak to them, inside where his men would no doubt eavesdrop, or outside where all of Sweet Pea might? "Keep the crew out of my hair."

Ash nodded. "And the neighborhood welcoming committee?" he asked, glancing at the two older men who had their eye on the investigators getting out of the car.

Bell wasn't wild about the idea for a number of reasons. The one he was willing to admit to was that they were not the intimidating loners with easily influenced minds he'd been hoping for. The one he was trying to ignore was the fact that Josie was friendly with them, and he knew she'd chew his ear off if they were hurt.

"Could they be useful?" Bell asked instead.

"A lawyer in the DA's office, and a member of the local planning committee? Yes, that could come in handy," Ash said.

"Sign 'em up," Bell said, stifling his own objections. "At least they have good taste in beer."

The door opened, and the detectives walked in, Cornell close on their heels.

"Gentlemen," Bell greeted without a smile. "I believe you're here to see me."

He led the detectives to the back booth, digging through their heads on the slow walk. They planned on checking his shoe size against the men's 11 print they'd found in the woods—easy, he'd given himself well above that for a good thud to his stride as he walked—but mostly they wanted to see if his story matched with Josie's version of their date.

Date.

He practically tripped over his own feet as the word landed in his head. That hadn't been what she'd said in Gunney's last night. He could hear the word in her voice, all sweetened as she lied through her teeth. And the uglier of the two, Crowley, kept replaying a particular comment of hers. They'd 'fooled around' she'd said, shrugging, and in the Sergeant's mind the words held an image of Bell and Josie on the ground together, rutting like animals in heat, a heavier attention to detail on Josie than Bell appreciated in anyone's mind but his own.

He swallowed his growl and sank into the back of the booth.

"Can we get your name for our records?" Detective Bagley asked. "No one seems to know it properly."

"Beleth King," Bell said, immediately blurring the thought in their minds so they wouldn't be able to look him up later. And while he was there... Bell took the image of Josie's head thrown back, eyes squeezed shut and lips parted on a pant, right out of Crowley's head. "But everyone calls me 'Bell.'"

Crowley frowned, eyes turning distant on the wall over Bell's head, and Bell tightened his fists at his sides. Then he went ahead and blurred Josie in Crowley's head so thoroughly that the Sergeant couldn't really recall if she was tall or short, or even what color her hair was.

It was an easy interview from there, they thought of Josie's answers to their questions, practically delivering Bell the right things to say. What worried him was that they were less interested in whether he and Josie had killed the ranger, then if he was lying for Josie. They'd already started forming a theory around her in particular.

Let them, a voice whispered in his head, but it didn't feel like his own so he brushed it away.

"And did you hear anything unusual or suspicious while you were out?" Bagley asked, already adjusting his theory away from Josie and onto the stitch witch.

"Josie did on our way out, but nothing came of it."

Bagley seemed satisfied. Crowley was more determined. "What time did you leave Josie at her apartment?"

Beleth paused long enough to make sure he wasn't about to contradict anything Josie said, and then he grinned, slow and satisfied. "I never said I left. We got back a bit after midnight."

Bagley stiffened, and Crowley smirked right back at Bell. *This* was a man they could use for their cause, Bell realized. Crowley would do their work beautifully. In fact, if Bell let him continue to pursue Josie as a suspect it would deal a serious blow to the town.

"Your bike was spotted on the way out of the alley shortly after," Crowley said.

Damn. He'd been digging with too much focus on Josie's story rather than all the information they'd gathered.

Bell conjured a laugh and a shrug. "Ah well. Can't blame a man for dreaming."

"In the future," Bagley started, and then frowned as he realized he couldn't remember Bell's name. "In the future, stick with the facts when it comes to the investigation. We'll be in touch again, I'm sure."

Bell followed the pair back to the doors, before stopping and joining Cornell and Thurman at the bar. Barbie was behind the counter, glowering as usual, but he'd drummed up bottles of IPA from somewhere, and appeared as content as he could be to listen to the couple reminisce on their days in a touring motorcycle crew.

Cornell paused in his story as Bell took a seat on the barstool next to him. The petite man turned to face Bell, eyes scanning him in study and lips pursing.

"I can give you the same name I gave Josie if you'd like. You should lawyer up if they ask for another interview," Cornell said.

Bell grunted. "You know why they're so focused on Josie for this?"

Cornell hummed and shrugged. "Oh, you know," he said, waving a hand. "This is a small town and those girls don't bother hiding their hobbies. Witchcraft is cute until some local yahoo thinks it's aiming to kill their crops or bring bad luck. Then it's Satanism."

Barbie made a huffing sound Bell thought might've been laughter.

"Of the four of them, they really oughta be looking at the Byrne sisters, but those girls are old family around here and Josie's *not*, which is what really gets people seeing trouble in places like this," Thurman said.

"June and Imogen are *not* murdering folk in the woods," Cornell tossed back at his husband. He turned back to Bell and raised his eyebrows. "All I'm saying is, if Josie's name is cleared, you lot will be next on the chopping block, so get yourself a good defense."

"Noted," Bell said with a dip of his head.

Cornell's shoulders shimmied as he sat up straighter. "Good. Now, what do Thu and I have to sign in blood to get ourselves some of those nasty looking jackets y'all wear. I would just *love* to roll up to the farmer's market in one of those. Really ruffle some dusty feathers round here."

Barbie huffed again, and Bell glanced sideways at him. Either the taciturn demon had a cold, or he liked the new recruits. Fair enough, Bell didn't mind them so much either.

———

"Where the hell is Vinny?" Bell growled, carrying a keg of black coffee porter on his shoulder up to the bar the next night.

They were meant to be having a toast to their new members—unlikely as they were in Bell's mind—but the new members were still missing. And Vinny, who Bell had ordered to rustle up a few waitresses to introduce to the club, was equally missing.

"Dunno, but there's some kind of activity happening on the street," Pie announced, passing the front windows.

Bell slid the keg into place under the bar, and glanced up at Pie who had stopped at the front door, eyes fixed onto the street over the top of his glasses. "An event?" Bell asked. Some kind of chintzy fall thing, no doubt. Probably with pumpkin carving. Festivities were disgusting.

"No…" Pie said, brow furrowing. Then he leaned on the door, opening it to a cool evening breeze. The sound of sirens called through the air, followed by the murmurs of locals on the street.

Danny and the others came out of the kitchen, Ash dropping off another keg behind the counter, all of them staring out the door.

"Another murder?" Dante asked.

"What?" Danny jumped at the question and ran for the door, squeezing out past Pie. He stopped on the sidewalk, gawking down the street, and Bell felt a pit forming in his stomach. "Everyone's down in front of the Bakery."

Bell's shoulder collided with Ash's as he rushed out from behind the bar to the front door, the others following close behind. Pie was trailing after Danny down the sidewalk, but Bell was on a beeline straight across the block, until he realized that the spectacle wasn't at Josie's but on the opposite side of the street. He slowed down, searching the heads in the crowd until two people shuffled closer together, and he caught sight of her. Josie stood in the heart of the onlookers, eyes wide and fixed on the storefront of Love & Lattes, her hand cupped over her open mouth.

The crowd on the street continued to shift around Josie, until Bell realized they were falling back from her, their stares turning away from the cafe—closed for the night—to the kitchen witch amongst them. Finally, Bell spared a glance for the building. The cafe sported a bright neon sign in their main window, and Bell squinted as a dark silhouette squirmed around the heart of the 'O' on 'Love'. He walked closer, jaw tightening as the view inside became clearer.

Snakes, dozens upon dozens, curling around the backs of chairs and slithering over countertops. A red fox scrabbling inside the window, raccoons in the pastry case at the counter. The inhabitants of the preserve, somehow trapped inside of the locked cafe, screeching and chittering and hissing at the audience on the street. An audience which was slowly turning to Josie, to stare at her out of the corner of their eyes. As if they thought *she* was capable of something like this.

Bell knew exactly where the blame lay. "Vinny," he snarled under his breath as a raccoon on a shelf knocked down a mason jar full of loose leaf tea, glass shattering on the floor.

"No!" moaned a middle aged woman, closest to the front of the cafe. She had keys fisted in her hands.

"Animal control is on their way, hun," a man said, wrapping an arm around her shoulder.

"They're destroying the shop," the woman whimpered, turning into his chest.

Pie arrived at Bell's left, Ashtaroth on his right. "They're looking at the witches," Ash murmured.

The stitch witch and her eerie sister had arrived, flanking Josie's sides much the way Bell's demons did him.

"The witches are looking at *us*," Pie said as Imogen's head whipped in their direction, her eyes sharp and narrowed. "It's Vinny's mark, they'll be able to tell."

Bell was less concerned with the witches knowing Vinny was responsible, than he was with the way the town was looking at Josie. Or the fact that Imogen was leaning in, whispering in her ear, clutching at Josie's arm. When Josie looked at him, her stare pierced right through Bell's gut, anger tightening her gaze against his. She blamed him, whether it was Vinny's handiwork or not.

And she should, he thought. He should've reined Vinny in from the start.

No. He should have celebrated Vinny's work. He should've enjoyed the way the town was turning on Josie Benoit. He should've been grinning at her, enjoying the strike of betrayal she was feeling. Maybe Vinny had done him a favor with this act of rebellion, turning her against him. If she was angry, it might be easier to resist the urge to seek her out, tease her and flirt with her.

But rebellion was rebellion, and he was going to take a special kind of pleasure in answering Vinny's.

"Close the Inferno," Bell said, words rumbling out in a whisper from his throat. "I'll be at the house."

He hunted for his leash on the wayward demon of his crew, found it trailing through town, and wrapped it up in a tight mental fist. He walked to his bike, mounting it and riding away from the scene on the street. Vinny thrashed against the chokehold Bell had on his willpower, dragging Vinny all the way to Grimsby House, practically feeling Vinny's heels scuffing on the ground as he rode.

Bell pulled into the driveway and walked around to the back of the house. The woods butted up against the delicately manicured rose bushes and herb beds of the house gardens, and Bell could hear twigs cracking and the soft muttered curses in demonic tongue as he reeled Vinny in with ruthless speed.

"What the fuck do you *want*?" Vinny snarled as he came skidding through the briars of a rose bush, collapsing to his knees in front of Bell.

Bell stared down at the other King with a brief and shallow satisfaction. Vinny looked haggard. The demand of Bell's pull through the granted link had cost Vinny some color and breath, even in his disguise.

"In a minute. First, tell me what you want, Vinny. Because by Beelzebub's sac, I can't seem to measure it out," Bell purred. Vinny's jaw locked shut, and Bell nodded, sliding his hands into his pockets and rolling back on his heels. "I have guesses, you know? You want to piss me off. You want to prove yourself as a superior demon. You want my position."

Vinny glared up at him, eyes flashing acidic green for a moment. "None of those sound *terrible*," he said.

Bell grinned, and a soft laugh curled out. "Have you ever met Morningstar, Vinny?" Vinny was quiet and Bell smiled. "I thought not. I assume you would like to? It's a great honor. You've served the cause for millennia. Even with your granted Kingship, I'm sure you've had to crawl around in the Bowels to get any due granted to you, just like the rest of us. A title doesn't offer much in the way of pride down there, does it?"

"Get to your fucking point," Vinny hissed.

"My point is that if you met Morningstar," Bell said, taking slow steps forward, "Your master would crush you for sticking a pinky toe out of line. Morningstar would burn you to cinders for daring to think an independent thought outside of the orders you were granted." Bell stopped directly in front of Vinny, mentally wrapping that leash around the other demon's arms and chest. He reached out, wrapping his hand around Vinny's throat, finding it convincingly fragile just like a human's would be. "I may be a more lenient leader than Morningstar, but that should not leave you feeling comfortable, Vine."

Bell tightened his grip about Vinny's throat, watching his fingers mark a pale trace of his grip, and Vinny's face turn red.

"Who told you to play games in town?" Bell snarled, enjoying the feel of Vinny's attempt to swallow, muscle flexing under the pressure of his thumb.

"We've wasted days here," Vinny squeezed out.

"*Whose orders were you following*?" Bell shouted, spittle flying into Vinny's electric green eye.

"No one's," Vinny mouthed, voice strangled.

"Then why did you do it?" Bell whispered, knowing there would be no answer. He stared fixedly at Vinny's face, watching eyes flutter shut, mouth gaping. Vinny squirmed, but Bell's grip was complete. "From now on, you breathe when I tell you to, step where I point your foot, and keep your cursed ideas in your head until I permit you to act."

Vinny's pulse thrummed under Bell's fingers, like a bird beating its wings inside a new cage, until finally it died. Bell dropped the demon to the ground, body landing with a dull smack against the grass. The stares of the rest of the crew were on his back as he stood straight. And against his cheek... Bell turned his head and saw the green witch looking out the window of the second story of her little carriage house. She would report the scene to her coven, but Vinny would be up again as soon as Bell decided he could tolerate the sulking, so there was no real risk in her witness.

He stomped any flicker of wonder about what Josie would think out of his head and turned to face the others.

"He'll be up in a few hours," he said, eyeing them. Pie and Ash would have no issue with his discipline, he knew that much. And Dante was smirking. Barbie and Aim were harder to read and newer to his service, but they didn't look angry or disturbed. "Take him inside," he said to Barbie, waiting to see what flickered across the demon's face.

Nothing. Not so much as a blink. Barbie and Aim strode forward, lifting Vinny's body between them and hauling it to the patio doors. Ash and Dante followed them in, and Bell caught a laugh from Dante's throat. Pie waited for Bell to join him.

"His actions served our purpose," Pie said, more an observance than a condemnation.

"Yes. But they weren't under my orders," Bell said. "If someone wants to be clever, they can clear it with me first."

Pie blinked. "Alright. It will be a reprieve from his huff-ing, at least."

Bell rolled his shoulders, finding a surprising tension lingering there, and followed Pie inside.

18

No Rude Man

Josie bit her lip, staring out the shop window of the bakery as John and Linda Love dragged out a third bag of trash from the wreckage of Love & Lattes' evening infestation. She'd watched from her living room window last night as Animal Control worked on retrieving the woodland menagerie out of the shop until well after midnight. What was left behind was a huge mess, and a guarantee that Love & Lattes wouldn't be cleared to open again until a thorough scrub down had been completed, not to mention all the ruined furnishings and stock.

Josie sucked in a deep breath and smoothed down her apron, crossing to the front door of her bakery and shoving open the door, bells clanging overhead.

Linda was standing at the corner of Love & Lattes as John threw the bag into the back of a dumpster the town had let them park on the street for the day. The exhausted woman's eyes glazed over Josie as she approached, before doubling back and widening.

"Hey," Josie said, jogging across the empty street. "I'd like to help, anyway I can."

Linda Love's lips pursed, and she flicked a hand at Josie in dismissal. "That ain't necessary."

"But it's neighborly," Josie said, shrugging. She offered a rare smile, tried to be Rosa with all her warmth and impervious charm. "I've got the espresso and coffee makers that I can lend you as long as you need. If they got into your stock, I'd be happy to share. I always over order the basics anyway."

Linda ran her tongue over her teeth behind her lips, and looked Josie up and down out of the corner of her eye. She was turned to where John leaned against the dumpster catching his breath, refusing to face Josie directly.

"If y'all need a nightshift to clean tonight—" Josie started again.

"I don't think you need to do this," Linda said, flat and terse. "You showed up here. Put yourself in competition with a local cafe as soon as you arrived. You made yourself clear."

Local. Like Josie was some kind of major chain out of the city. "I never considered us in competition," she said, trying to find peace.

Linda clucked and swiveled to face her, dark lined eyebrows raised high on her forehead. "Didn't you? Well bless your heart, but we sure as hell felt it, honey. A hoity toity little bakery that just *happens* to offer espresso? Right *across* the street from us."

"It was the only space available," Josie said, voice growing high and anxious.

"In *this* town," Linda growled back. "We have managed since you got here. We will manage now that you've... that this *strange phenomenon* has happened, and our doors will be open just as soon as they can be. So really, sweetheart," she said, the word loaded with any flavor but sweet, "Don't you worry a second about us."

There were folk out on the sidewalk, and since the murders had caught some attention on the news, their audience was mainly local. It was time to retreat.

"If you change your mind, let me know," Josie murmured, turning away.

Her heart was pounding in her ears, hot shame licking like flames up her face. Worse, she found Bell waiting outside the bakery as she stumbled across the road, his eyes narrowed on the Loves.

"What do you want?" she asked, words all choked up in her throat. She didn't wait for his answer, tearing open the door and rushing back behind her counter as if it was a barricade between her and the suspicious town. Behind her, Bell's feet landed softly on her tile, chimes gentling as the door closed behind them.

She spun to face him, hands bracing on her counter. "Was it you?" she asked, even though Imogen had told her it was the work of Vinny.

He shook his head.

It wasn't a relief. "Was it your orders?"

"No," he said, hands shoving into his pockets. He held her stare, and it was somehow worse, this lack of shame on his part.

You wanted the demon to feel shame? Stupid Josie, she thought.

"It doesn't matter. This is what you're here to do. Turn this town in on itself. I am a good mark," she said, nodding as if she approved of the plan, jutting her chin forward. "Easy starter plate for them to swallow."

Bell didn't say a word, and Josie thought she might like to throw a plate at his head. This was her fault. For trusting him. Or maybe not that much, but for *liking* him.

"What do you want?" she asked.

He opened his mouth, grimaced, and shut it again before his eyes flicked over to her pastry case. "Quiche?" he said, sounding not quite sure.

"No," she snapped. Bell straightened, grew larger in front of her door, glowered at her. Fuck that, she was not going to be scared of him, no matter what he was or what he got this town to believe about her. "Get out of my shop, Bell. Don't come back here."

She would make sure he couldn't step within three feet of the door if she had to. Imogen would know how, if she couldn't find the answer herself.

Bell glared across the store front at her, as if he were trying to communicate something to her without saying it out loud. Except he was a demon, and if he wanted to do that she was pretty sure he could. Josie held her breath, glared right back, and a moment later Bell turned heel and left. Her phone blared in her pocket, making her jump, and Josie dug it out to see Rosa's name.

"What did he want?" Rosa asked in a rush over the phone. Figures Josie's friends were spying on her. Not that she minded so much. Rosa would back her up if Josie needed her.

"Quiche," Josie spat.

"Did he apologize?"

Had she been very transparent this whole time about her attraction to the demon? "Why would he do that?"

"I saw him last night. Imogen said it was Vinny that put that little display on at L&L's? Well, Bell choked Vinny to death...to temporary death, at least. Looked like a punishment, not a reward for good work."

A little bubble of hope swelled in her chest, and Josie stamped it out with every last ounce of emotional strength she possessed. Unfortunately, after the past two weeks she was lacking in her reserves, and what remained was small but persistent.

"He's a demon. We *know* why they're here. He's not on my side. None of them are on anyone's side but their own. And maybe not even that," she said, shrugging.

Rosa hummed. "Okay. I just... I mean, I get it, babe. I really do. And you're right, and I shouldn't say this..." Rosa rushed on, "But I'm gonna anyways, and I think that he looks at you in a not-his-enemy kind of way, and that maybe he came to check on you or something. I dunno. It could all be an act."

"It could be an act," Josie agreed. "The bad boy look is all well and good, but I'm not interested in the psyche of a demon, okay?" She was, a bit. This demon, anyway.

"Okay," Rosa said, and Josie could practically hear her friend nodding. "I love you, you're a strong woman, and you don't need no rude man."

"No rude men," Josie agreed. "I could use, like, a girls' night. *In*," she added. She didn't need to go back to Gunney's again to be stared at.

"Wine," Rosa offered.

"Rum," Josie said, thinking of her Loa spirits. "And magic."

"I'll text the others."

THE DAY DRAGGED on and Josie frowned at her case of pastries, snacking aimlessly off her own product. If no one was going to buy it, then a lot of her fucking work was going to waste, and that made her angry *and* hungry. If she was sick off sugar by closing time, Sweet Pea could take the blame.

The bells on her door finally sang as she was beating some puff pastry into submission for the weekend's croissants, and Josie stepped back to see who had arrived.

Wandering closer to her counter was Richard Merryweather, wearing the same frumpy waist coat he'd had on at the county forum last week.

"Be right with you," she called.

Merryweather froze in place, eyes darting to find her. His expression reminded her of a rabbit still on the road in the glow of headlights, but a smile wobbled out after a long pause. Josie rewrapped her pastry and tucked it back into the fridge, wiping her hands on her apron.

"How can I help you?" she asked, walking up to the counter. He was her only customer of the day. She hadn't had a day this slow since she'd decided to be open during a level two snow storm in case any stranded tourists wanted drinking chocolate and warm pastry. Actually, today was worse than that day, because a couple of stranded tourists *had* wandered in during the snow storm.

"I... um..." he swallowed and bent forward studying her case. She caught the tell tale growth of his gaze and then blink of shock as he noted her prices.

"Half-off everything," she said. "Slow day."

He nodded and glanced at her out of the corner of his eye. "Heard some funny things about you when I got into Sweet Pea today."

Josie tried not to crack a tooth with the grinding of her jaw and just nodded. "Bet you did. Been that kinda week. I'm still the new girl in town, five years later."

"And those bikers," he said. "One of them is your man, isn't he?"

Well damn, Merryweather had heard the whole kit and caboodle, hadn't he? And he sure was chatty about it.

"No," she said. "Just one date. Not my type."

It came down to him being a mythical, shitty species. And also an asshole.

"I...I don't really believe much of what people say," Merryweather murmured.

Was he going to order or not? Josie summoned patience with a slow breath in. He was a customer, or he would be if he ordered, and he was also a man stuck on his own up on a mountain farm. She imagined that made him a little starved for talk.

"Everyone keeps saying they'll vote to keep the preserve, but I know that ain't true," he said, rising and giving her a limpid smile.

Josie huffed a laugh. "I'm planning on voting to keep it as well," she said, grinning.

For some reason, that seemed to distress Merryweather, and he paled as he blinked at her. "It doesn't matter much," he said, voice stammering. "I'll be leaving the area soon. The family name has lost its worth around here anyway."

"That's a shame," Josie said. "It's hard to pull your roots up, and I bet yours go deep 'round here."

The bells over Josie's door rang again before Richard could answer, and Josie's eyebrows ticked up on her forehead as Imogen walked in. *Unaccompanied by June. That's unusual*, Josie thought.

"Hey there," Josie said.

"I came for girls' night," Imogen offered in greeting. Then she floated past Josie right back to the kitchen without asking.

Richard took in a deep breath, his eyes tracking Imogen, and the sound was shaky and wet in his chest, and then he glanced between Josie and her case again.

"I'll have a brownie," he said, adding on in a rush, "To go."

Josie rang him up. She wanted to feel sympathy for the man, she really did. Thinking about packing up his life here, his entire family's history of life, had to be heart wrenching. But she had her own troubles to worry about, and right now she just wanted to close up the shop and get into her apartment with her coven.

"Hope you enjoy," she said, passing him his brownie. He tucked his change into his pocket, ignoring her tip jar, and Josie's smile faltered. That was alright, she told herself. Lots of people ignored the tip jar. "And I hope you don't let the vote, no matter how it comes out, sway your decision on whether or not to stick around here."

Merryweather's head bobbed on his shoulders, not a nod really, more like a tic, and he shuffled quickly to her door, opening it just as Rosa appeared. He pushed past her and Rosa rolled her eyes and stepped inside, bringing the scent of lavender and jasmine in with her. She was wearing a voluminous baby blue vintage nightgown beneath a brown leather jacket and had on red rain boots. Just the sight of her made Josie's shoulders relax.

"He was my only customer today," Josie said, after the door had shut on him.

Rosa's nose wrinkled. "I gotta be honest. That man gives me the heebie jeebies. Seems like one of those Appalachian incest families."

"I think those are rumors," Josie said. She tipped her head and watched Merryweather get into his car, pulling out onto the street before remembering to turn his headlights on. "But he is a little odd," she admitted.

Imogen reappeared from the kitchen, Josie's box of

discarded pastry cradled in her arms and crumbs at the corner of her lips.

"Hey Imogen, didn't see you there," Rosa said with quirked lips. "Come on. Close up and let's go curl up upstairs with spiced rum and tarot cards. June'll be over as soon as she closes."

Josie nodded and started to close out her register as Rosa locked her front door for her. The longer she stared at the screen, the more the numbers blurred and her eyes stung.

"Hey. Hey, what's going on?" Rosa asked, curling up to Josie's side and wrapping an arm around her shoulders. Rosa was almost a full head taller than her friend, and she tucked Josie's head beneath her chin. Imogen stepped closer but she felt more like an observer than another friend offering comfort.

"Do you know how fast I could go out of business if this keeps up?" Josie said, squeezing the words out of her tight throat. "Even if they find the murderer—the whole thing with Love & Lattes, everyone *wants* to think it was witchcraft."

"Only because of the ritual sites in the woods," Rosa said, kissing the top of Josie's head. That was going to leave a lipstick print in the hardest to find place. "Trust me. They find the killer and everyone's gonna be back on our side again. Or at least not against us. And I've got savings—"

"Don't you dare," Josie said.

"—So I can make a business loan to you if necessary," Rosa finished.

"I have some inheritance left," Imogen said.

Josie growled, but it sounded a little pitiful, and Rosa only kissed the prickly soft surface of her head again. "Neither of you is putting money into a sinking ship. These are worries for tomorrow. Let's pack up all this food and gorge ourselves on booze and pastry."

Rosa hissed with excitement, bouncing behind Josie to the case and immediately popping a macaron into her mouth. Imogen followed suit, offering Josie a strange kind of smile, and then went about filling the box in her arms with an assortment of Josie's best offerings.

19 · THE BLESSING OF A NON-BELIEVER

Josie narrowed her eyes at Danny and looked at his handwritten order.

"Is it... too much?" he asked.

A few days had passed, and Love & Lattes was almost back up and running, the full support of Sweet Pea behind them. Meaning almost the full support of Sweet Pea had been absent from Josephine's Bakery. Thankfully, Cornell was making an almost daily catering order for the DA's office and one of the local B&Bs had a daily order for her pastries at breakfast. Turns out, she wasn't the only business in town that felt the cold shoulder of the historic Sweet Pea families.

"It's not too much," Josie said, following the long trail of desserts. "I didn't know the Inferno wanted a dessert menu."

"Some of it's just for the guys, I think," Danny said. His eyes widened as he added, "They can eat *a lot.*"

Yeah, she bet demons had an appetite. She bet they didn't even know the word 'calories' either. Just another reason to resent them.

Oh, how she wanted to refuse their business. But this amount of money would take care of her bills. It would keep her doors open. It would probably help cover lawyer bills too, if it came to that. And either Inferno was planning on putting serious price tags on their dessert menu or taking zero profit, because they hadn't asked for a discount at all.

'They.' More like *Bell*. Rosa had asked if he gave her an apology, and now Josie wondered if this was his version of one. She *preferred* one face to face, but this wasn't so bad.

"Pick up is at ten AM, sharp. I don't have the storage to hold onto everything for you guys," Josie said, because for the sake of her principles, she was at least going to be a little prickly about this exchange. It was partly their damn fault no one wanted to eat her food anymore. She wasn't going to *thank* Bell.

"Um, okay, and these are for my sister," Danny said, passing her a smaller note that said 'easy to eat cookies for walk-ins.'

"Mona?" Josie asked. "I thought she was subbing at the school."

"Just got her art gallery together in the Cottage Around The Corner," he said, perking up with pride. The Cottage was a cute little local landmark that'd recently gone up for rent after operating as a doily infested gift-shop for decades.

"That's fantastic!" Josie said. "Hang on, let me put something together for her."

Mona was a sweetheart and discovered her opera cake addiction on day one of Josephine's opening. Josie assumed the rumor mill scared the woman off recently, but if Mona was putting her art gallery together, that explained her absence. Josie hurried back to the kitchen and found her box of imperfects. Generally she would gift them to anyone she ran into at the end of the day, but since that list of people had shrank this week, and her coven was now fully stocked on sweets, this was the perfect opportunity.

She returned to her counter and boxed up an additional slice of opera cake. "That's for your sister," Josie said, passing the two boxes across the counter. "Tell her to let me know which of those cookies fly first, and I'll sell her a batch at cost whenever she needs them. These are on the house today. A gallery opening present."

Danny smiled and then frowned in quick succession. "That's awesome, but...um, I think she wanted to—"

"She can pay next time," Josie said, waving a hand. She tapped her finger against the order for Inferno and added, "I'm good, honestly."

Danny looked so genuinely cheered to hear it, that it bled into Josie as well, followed quickly by a sinking dread.

"Hey, so... what do those guys have you doing, anyway?" she asked. Danny was a good kid, and while she couldn't tell him to quit hanging out with *demons,* and it seemed a little cliche to warn him off of bikers, she at least wanted to make sure they weren't dragging Danny down with them.

His face lit up. "I'm the head chef! It's awesome. Bell literally doesn't give a shit what I feel like making, as long as it's edible."

Josie snorted at the description. "I dunno if that's the best advertisement for your food," she teased.

Danny blushed, but his chest puffed up. "You'll just have to come and find out. I'm gonna surprise this town!"

Josie grinned and nodded. "I look forward to it. Ten AM tomorrow, yeah?"

"Yeah," Danny agreed, bouncing on the balls of his feet. "See you then, Josie."

Josie bit her smile off as the door swung shut behind Danny. She tried to tamp down the warm feeling building inside of her. It was nice to know who in this town was willing to go out of their way to support her through this mess, but she needed to remember why Bell and his men were here. They could be helping her just to piss the town off.

Her smile was wobbling away as her door opened again, and June came inside.

"Hey, what's up?"

"Taking a lunch break," June said. "Can I buy some quiche and run an idea by you?"

"Of course," Josie said, going to slice herself a piece of butternut sage quiche as well.

"I want us to do a warding spell on Samhain," June said as Josie brought out their dishes on a tray, including coffee for them both. "It'll be one of the last chances we'll have for working in Merryweather Preserve."

Josie winced, her fork hovering over the food. "Do you really think that's a good idea? Considering the climate of the town at the moment?"

"I think we should invite the town to join us," June said.

Josie stiffened, staring across the table at an impenetrable June. "Are you being serious? That's..."

"Totally inappropriate to a circle, I know," June said, which was *not* what Josie was thinking. "But if they were there, if we worked protection magic *transparently* in front of them, it might help reassure them that we only care for this town. We aren't the ones causing any of the harm."

Josie's lips pursed. "And it might help prevent any more trouble from traveling into town. Hell's Bells, could it..."

June shook her head. "I don't think it would banish them. But if they had something in motion, we might be able to feel the resistance of our ward. It would give us a heads up at least."

Josie chewed on the tines of her fork. "Let me think about it?"

June nodded. "I came to you first. If you're comfortable with it, we'll talk to Rosa and Imogen. In the meantime, I'll plan the spell."

"What would it take to banish them?" Josie asked, pushing a bite of quiche around her plate, her heart cold in her chest.

"The demons?" June murmured, and Josie nodded. "Something stronger. And less charming if we have an audience. Imogen would know."

"I think we should be prepared for that," Josie said.

June stared out the window in the direction of Inferno, and Josie mulled over the suggestion. It might mean her business collapsed to chase the demons out of town at this point. And maybe that's what Bell wanted, for her to need him too much to fight him. If that was the case, he underestimated her love of Sweet Pea. The town might not love her back at the moment, but that wasn't their fault. And the demons were right, this was a *good* place. It deserved to have people looking after it, and she would be one of those people if she could.

"Alright," June said. "I'll talk to Imogen."

WITH THE ORDER for Inferno in place, Josie stayed in the kitchen well after closing, folding and rolling butter into her puff pastry, prepping her chocolate into fine shavings, and mixing doughs to chill. She hurt from head to toe in a way she hadn't since the early days of opening the shop, all her muscles screaming for rest. A long, steaming bath was in order, with one of Rosa's homemade herbal bath bombs and little candles on the ledge. The whole works.

Josie smiled as she locked the back door of the kitchen,

and then shuffled over to her apartment door. The lock snicked as she turned her key, but her ears rang as she stepped inside. Someone was here, in her apartment. She frowned, thinking of Bell. Had he figured out how to hide his presence from her and tried to sneak in for a second time?

She tip-toed up the stairs, waiting to hear the shuffle of boots on the floor, to catch that hint of smoke on the air that followed Bell. Arguments ran through her head, how to kick him out of her apartment, tell him he couldn't buy her acceptance of his crew's presence in town. Equally, and shamefully, the words came to tease him for trying to sneak in again.

When she found the living room and kitchen empty, and looked down the hall to her bedroom, seeing the warm glow of candlelight, expectation turned into anxiety. Bell's name was on her tongue, but she was less certain it was him waiting in that room. What if one of the other demons had snuck in? She was halfway to her bedroom when she realized she should be heading right back out the front door and downstairs to call the police.

One step back, her heel connecting with the floor, and the old floorboards betrayed her, creaking ominously. Josie held her breath for all of a beat, and her bedroom door swung inwards, whoever was waiting inside just behind it. She turned tail and started running for the door, heartbeat pounding in her ears. Footsteps echoed after hers, vibrating under her own feet, and Josie didn't care if it *was* Bell. She didn't care if she'd let him terrorize her into running. Better that than the alternative.

When an arm banded around her waist, and another around her throat, Josie screamed, the sound cut off almost immediately by the way the crook of her attacker's elbow squeezed against her neck. She was lifted off the ground, thrashing and kicking at the body behind her as they carried her backwards into her bedroom.

Josie's breath died in her chest as she was spun around, finally seeing the disaster of her bedroom. Her altar had been dismantled for the second time this month, candles torn out of place and arranged in a large circle in the open area of her bedroom. A crooked chalk circle was ground into her floorboards, familiar symbols scratched through. For a moment, she thought it was the demons, that it'd been them all along, and somehow Bell had pulled a massive trick on her. She was going to kill him. She promised herself that much. And then she was thrown to the floor outside of the circle with a body pouncing on her, knees in her back, and the memory of the woods rising up in her like the bile in her throat.

She tried to pull herself away, but her hands were caught up, sticky adhesive wrapping around her wrists to the tell-tale sound of a roll of duct tape being unravelled.

"Get off," Josie cried, shoulders bucking, even as she knew the words were useless.

Hands gripped her arms, and then she was rolled over, staring up into the red and sweating face of Richard Merry-weather.

"Wha-? What are you doing?" She was arched uncom-fortably, her arms bound behind her back, body twisted and legs pinned beneath Merryweather's knees.

"I'm sorry," he said, frowning, a thin line of spit shining down his chin. "I only meant to find out if you- if you'd seen me that night. If you remembered."

Josie gaped, chest heaving. The night in the woods. It had been Merryweather! *All* of it had been Merryweather, aside from Love & Lattes.

"I didn't, I didn't know!" Josie cried, trying to squirm away, but he was at least twice her size. And she knew now.

"Everyone already thinks it's you," Merryweather rasped. "They think you did it. And if I just make it look right... They'll just think you were crazy."

Josie had never realized how hearing herself spoken of in past tense could be so utterly chilling.

"I don't understand," Josie whispered. The chalk circle was in the corner of her eye, and she glanced at it. "You're not... it wasn't really about demons was it?"

Had Merryweather brought Bell and the others somehow? But no, he scoffed and grabbed Josie's thighs in both his hands, turning her and dragging her closer to the circle.

"I thought it would spook people, didn't know there were- that you lot think you're..." he scoffed again and shook his head, spiraling tape around her ankles. He crossed to her altar next, grabbing up one of Josie's ceremonial knives, and she whimpered and tried to worm away, knowing she'd never make it far enough to escape.

Merryweather shoved her onto her back again as he returned to her, tucking the blade of the knife up beneath the hem of her shirt. Josie held her breath and swallowed a sob as he sliced upwards, cutting through her shirt from navel to throat, pushing it aside and revealing her plain black bra.

"If the land is going to sell, it should come back to *me*," he said. "The buyer is scared off. And the votes were never going to be on my side. But I should be able to afford the land again now, after the murders."

"Murders you committed!" Josie snapped, her head pounding with panic, mood sliding wildly through every emotion. Terror, anger, annoyance, a desperate hope for pity.

Merryweather only nodded, lined eyes sliding shut and sloped shoulders sagging. "I just meant to spook those kids."

"Liar," Josie whispered, and his eyes flashed open to fix to hers. "You're a liar," she repeated, voice croaking. "You went right for them. They didn't even get a chance to *look* at you."

His brow furrowed, and he stared hard at her face, the tension making the angles of his face sharpen into something predatory. "No one around here gives a shit about my family. We gave them every inch of the land they walk on, and they forgot about us."

Josie jutted her jaw forward and glared back at him. "Excuse my lack of sympathy."

The tip of the knife pricked her skin beneath her belly button, a warm bloom of blood welling up, and she gasped and collapsed again.

"I'm sorry," he whispered again, brow furrowed as he stared at her stomach. "I'd... I'd save this for later, but it has to look *right*. Like you carved the mark yourself before..."

"Please," Josie said, voice breaking, body trying to wriggle away from the tip of the knife poised above her ribcage. "Please don't."

With his free hand he reached into his back pocket, shaking out a sheet of paper that looked like it'd been printed off the internet. With the candlelight coming from the circle, Josie could see what was printed, glowing through the sheet; a black circle with a strange combination of lines and curls inside, and one upside down heart at the bottom. She could have laughed. It was Beleth's damn sigil.

"You're calling a demon?" she asked.

Merryweather gave her a sidelong glance of confusion, head tipping. He set the sheet down on the floor and then braced his hand over her lower stomach, the sweat of his palm an oily touch on her skin. "Demons aren't real," he said flatly.

The knife dug into her skin, and Josie screamed, forcing Merryweather's hand over her mouth. He drew the circle around the entirety of her stomach, and Josie found herself tightening her muscles and forcing herself to hold still for the assault.

After all, she really needed that sigil to come out right. Her life might depend on it.

20 · BLOOD AND PROMISES

Bell glared at the rescheduled crew party from his corner booth in Inferno. Dante and the others had conjured waitresses out of local girls, and Danny had found a collection of friends to help in the kitchen, from various restaurant jobs he'd held. Cornell and Thurman somehow managed to mingle with everyone, even Barbie, whose lips twitched every so often in the presence of the older men.

It was not the success of an introductory party for the crew that he'd originally hoped for. There were canapés instead of beer cans, and their recruits were grinning instead of glowering. It was possible that Sweet Pea was winning the battle they'd come to wage, twisting the dark intentions of the crew into some kind of camaraderie.

None of that was the reason for Bell's pissy mood.

He slid out from behind the booth, stalking up to the front door, narrowly avoiding an intentional collision with one of the eyelash batting waitresses. Dante would need to give those girls marching orders to stay out of his way. He wasn't interested in idle entertainment. At least not from them.

Pie joined him at the window and held out a beer bottle in offering.

"You look as though you need reminding of what we've accomplished," Pie said slowly. "Votes lean heavily to selling the Preserve. The witches are out of favor. When tourism picks up again, Inferno will wash two local businesses out."

Bell nodded and tried to ignore the heaviness in his chest. He was well aware of what had been done. It was the lack of pride in their progress that concerned him.

"This is *your* mission," Pie said in a whisper.

Bell turned to look at him, an eyebrow raised in question, trying to understand the secret in the words. Pie's lips parted to continue ,when a sudden yank in Bell's gut left him staggering, palm pressed to the window. The call faltered, and Bell frowned at his own reflection, eyes sliding up to stare crossways down the street to a golden window near the far corner.

"A summoning?" Pie asked.

It was weak, the flicker of vanilla faint, but enough to have Bell's tongue flick out against his lip craving more.

"You could resist it," Pie said.

Bell grinned. "I could. Call me curious."

Pie nodded. "Just don't let the humans see."

"Of course," Bell said, although he'd been just about to follow the call without giving a shit who might see him vanish.

He pushed outside and jogged across the street, savoring the call in his blood that tugged him to the alley. He might have walked the whole way there, just to leave her waiting for him, but his impatience won out. When he stepped into a dark spot of the alley, he gave up the hold of his control and spun into ether. He hadn't made up his mind on how to appear to Josie when he caught the first whiff of rich, metallic blood. His boots landed in the heart of a shoddily made summoning circle, body crouching and a wolf's muzzle baring his teeth in a snarl.

Josie was pinned to the floor by a human man, her eyes wide on Bell and full of relief and terror. Blood oozed over her stomach onto the floorboards, *his* mark carved into her skin in a way he found both satisfying and enraging. The man's head shot up, and Bell didn't care who he was, if he was faintly familiar or not. Identity was meaningless for a man who was seconds from deceased.

"What the hell?" the man breathed, body shaking as he gawped up at Bell.

"Smudge the circle," Bell growled to Josie.

She was pale and trembling, but she screamed behind the man's hand over her mouth and thrashed her bound legs out from under his, taking advantage of his shock at seeing Bell halfway transformed into a beast. Or maybe it was simply the impossibility of someone appearing out of nothing. Tears leaked out of Josie's eyes as she twisted so her feet scrubbed over the edge of the circle, and Bell grinned as soon as he felt the frail bubble of containment pop. He leapt across the space, knocking the man off Josie and to the floor, relishing the bite of pain under his own skin as he transformed his fingers into claws to tear the man apart.

"You can't kill him!" Josie cried out.

"I can, and I'll enjoy it," Bell growled.

"What are you?! What is this?" the man whimpered and shuddered beneath Bell. Just as Josie had trembled under him. Bell's vision was red with fury. She had been *hurt*, marked, frightened.

"He has to confess! Bell, if he doesn't confess, it'll all get blamed on me," Josie said, and Bell's skin shivered as he felt her resistance, the mark on her skin influencing his will.

He rumbled, swallowing a roar that ached to be released, and focused on the man's eyes. Merryweather. That's who this fucker was. Bell shook the claws out of his hands and wrapped a hand over Merryweather's forehead, pressing into his temples and striking him useless with magic. The body went limp beneath him, and some of the stinging fury in his blood eased at the sound of Josie's rattling sigh.

"Will... will he wake up again?" Josie asked, and Bell's fists clenched at the wobble in her tone.

"When I want him to," he said turning to face her. She was trying to sit up, and Bell climbed off Merryweather to help her, tearing through the tape around her ankles and where her wrists were bound behind her back. "Then he'll sing every second of the murders to the police."

"Good," Josie said, squaring her jaw and nodding. There was blood dripping down her stomach, staining her skin, and he reached his hands out to cover the mark, but she caught them in her own and held him back. "You can't heal me, Bell. It's proof. We need it."

He wanted to be sick, and Josie looked about two seconds from fainting. He tore his shirt off over the back of his head and pressed it to her skin, adding cool magic to cut through the pain. "Just to slow the bleeding," he muttered.

"Okay. Okay, we need to call the police," Josie murmured, wincing as she glanced down at Merryweather and then over at her blood on the floor, blending in with the scuffed white circle.

Enough, Bell thought, and he wrapped his hands around her shoulders and pulled her up from the floor, taking her out into the hall.

"He won't—"

"He won't wake until I want him to," he repeated.

Josie's feet tripped underneath her, and she tipped to the side, sliding down the wall. "Here's good. I don't wanna get blood on the couch."

Bell resisted the urge to mention he could get the blood out of the damn couch as long as she was *okay*, and crouched in front of her, blocking her view of her bedroom.

"There's a spare key to the apartment on top of the fridge," Josie said.

"So?"

"So go get it. I gave it to you, so you could show up when you wanted," Josie said, and when his brow furrowed, she added, "You know, that's how you got in tonight and caught Merryweather. Call the police, go downstairs, unlock the door, and leave it open a crack for them. We're dating or whatever, and you came over and caught him."

"Yeah, yeah. I got it," Bell said. How the hell was she thinking straight when she'd been carved up, and *he* was somehow incapable of stringing together a thought deeper than *Josie's hurt*? The spare key was overkill on the details, and he didn't even have a damn key ring, but he would *conjure* one if that was what she wanted.

"911, what's your emergency?"

Bell grunted through the explanation as he hurried down the stairs and cracked open Josie's door, before running back up. He knew Merryweather wasn't getting up again until Bell was good and ready to let him, but he didn't like leaving Josie while she was bleeding and still shaking with adrenaline and fear.

Admit it, a voice whispered inside of him.

Fuck you, I do admit it, Bell thought back. Josie *mattered*. Specifically, to him.

Her eyes were fixed on the bedroom door when he returned to the hallway, hands pressing his t-shirt to the wounds on her stomach.

"I was hoping you'd come," she said, and Bell blocked her view again, forcing her to meet his eyes. Her smile was weak. "I didn't know if you'd be on my side, though."

He wanted to say it, but the words were too heavy on his tongue. If he gave her those words, she deserved for them to be true and not just spoken in the moment. Eventually, he would have to perform his duty here in Sweet Pea, and there was no way to twist the situation that would benefit Josie.

Instead, he said, "Vinny acted against my orders at the cafe. He was punished." Josie's eyes blinked sluggishly, and she nodded. It wasn't blood loss, just the slow onslaught of shock. "I can force him to confess or—"

"Have Merryweather take the blame for it," she said.

"Done," Bell said, reaching through space and rearranging Merryweather's memories on the subject.

"Thank you," Josie whispered, and he rested his fingertips against her pulse, frowning to see the way he left bloody marks behind. "For coming," she added.

If he could've strangled himself, he might've tried, but nothing would restrain the words that followed.

"I won't let any harm come to you, Josie."

Her gaze flicked up to his, and the pain wrenching through his chest was indescribable but he relished it, it was a decent punishment for being so weak to fall under her sway. This witch would unravel his mission, Bell was fairly certain of it. At least his part in it. But the vow was made, and he intended to keep it.

Bell's head dipped as Josie's chin tipped up. She smelled of blood and butter and sugar, and they were the exact flavors he found on her bottom lip as he took it between his teeth, sucking on the flesh and soothing his tongue across the swell. One of Josie's hands reached up, claiming the back of his neck and tangling her fingers into his hair as she sighed against the kiss.

It wasn't enough. Bell surrounded her, grasping at her hips and dragging her up to his lap to twine around him like she had on that ride home on his bike. He stole tastes of her, his tongue against hers, her lips surrounded by his, their breath mingling. Josie's left hand was trapped between them, and he wondered how many of her whimpers and sighs where due to the pain of her wounds, so he stroked his hands up her bloody sides, numbing the sting and ache in the wake of his touch. She pulled his lip between her teeth, a fiercer nip then he'd served her, and Bell growled and pinned her to the wall. He hadn't let himself admire the view of her chest, practically bare, not when she was bleeding—but there was no stopping him from savoring the crush of her breasts against his chest and the hammer of her heart.

The kiss slowed and then dallied, and Bell softened, cradling Josie in his hold as if he could hold back the rest of the world, and keep the clock from ticking against them. Josie's nose nudged against his, and then her head fell back to the wall with a soft thud. Her lips were shining and swollen pink, and there was shock written in her gaze. Sirens rang in the alley. Bell thought they could try and pry him off her if they really wanted, but he had no plans on untangling her from around him.

"Merryweather," Josie whispered, and Bell focused on the way her tongue slicked against her bottom lip more than the warning. "You need to wake him up."

There went his plan to keep her clinging to him. Bell sighed and, to the surprise of them both, pressed another kiss to the corner of her mouth before sliding her off his lap and stalking to the bedroom. With a flick of his fingers it was Merryweather's turn to be trussed up in duct tape, body laying limp and unconscious.

Feet stomped on the stairs up to Josie's apartment, and Bell had seconds to wake Merryweather. Which was fine. He knew exactly how he wanted to do it. He stood over the body of the man, snarled at the sight of Josie's blood on his hands and shirt, and then drew back his arm and slammed his fist home, breaking Merryweather's nose with a satisfying crunch. The man woke with a whimpered shout and screamed as he saw Bell looming over him.

"I knew the vote would move to sell the land. I deserved that money—" Merryweather began immediately.

"Save it for the investigators," Bell said, and then he grabbed Merryweather by the collar and dragged him to the bedroom door, blowing the candles out at his back with a gust of conjured air.

SIRENS BLARED at Bell's back as he walked down the alleys and side streets of Sweet Pea. Josie was on her way to the hospital, and every step in the opposite direction felt as though a fishing line was unravelling in his chest, hook caught on the witch traveling farther and farther away.

It was all worse than he feared. Josie's sway over his thoughts could no longer be blamed on amusement. She mattered in a way he refused to consider too closely. As much as Morningstar and his role in Hell, perhaps. Bell could only think of one way of dealing with the situation.

Utter denial.

As he neared Grimsby House it became clearer. There would have to be two of him. One, the Warlord and Morningstar's axe. The other...

The other he still refused to put words to, but he knew it revolved around Josie Benoit.

21 COMPROMISE

Paimon listened to the soft scuffle of boots coming up the cobblestone drive, rolling a red tipped cigarette between his fingers but not smoking it. He'd been staring over the garden fence for the better part of an hour, in a patient meditation while Beleth was missing at the summoning of a witch. It concerned Pie that they'd been discovered by the witches, their goals laid bare. It concerned him even more that Bell didn't seem to mind.

His eyes flicked to the shadows under a red Sweetgum tree. Bell had *walked* back from the kitchen witch, and now he was...almost hiding.

Kings don't hide, Paimon thought, the judgement hard as stone in his head. He brushed it away as if it were sand, that old voice of his thoughts a tired thing now.

"That was a long summoning," Pie said, eyeing the shadow. "What did she want?"

Bell stepped out into the light, drifting slowly to the table, and Pie was disturbed by the unsettled look on Bell's face. The Warlord King wasn't angry, he wasn't smirking, he wasn't even stony and centered. Bell looked... brittle, and disturbingly human.

"I'm compromised," Bell said finally, checking to be sure no one in Grimsby House was paying attention to them.

Pie's feet slid off the seat across from him, and his spine straightened, smoke curling and obscuring his stare. "You're working against us?"

"No." Bell's jaw worked, and Pie caught a hint of sugar in the air before Bell seemed to draw it back in on himself.

"Are you... preventing us from performing the mission?" Pie asked.

"Shouldn't be a problem," Bell said.

Which meant it could be and wasn't yet.

"Do you *want* to be sent back?" Pie asked, head cocking.

"No."

Pie stared at Beleth, but his fellow King only stared back, firm in answer. "You said when things go wrong, it has to do with the team."

Finally, Bell smirked. "I did say that."

"What did she call you for?"

Bell shook his head. "She didn't. The murderer did, accidentally," and so the story came out, Pie's eyebrows ratcheting up with every word.

Beleth had protected the kitchen witch, had vowed her safety. No matter how he wanted to play the words, they were *made,* and Paimon wondered if Bell really understood the knot he'd tied himself in.

"Is this a game to play?" Pie asked, head tilting to the side. "Like Ash and the stitch witch? Are you gaining her trust?"

"Would I have told you I was compromised if it was?" Bell asked, voice dark and growling.

"I suppose not," Pie said. In fact, he suspected the situation was further developed than Bell admitted, if he was willing to speak of it at all.

"I'm not stepping down," Bell said. "I'm warning you, and *only* you. I'll let you know if it...gets more serious."

Send him to the Bowels, the voice in Pie's head bellowed. But Pie was...curious. Could Bell keep his promise to the witch? Was a human woman really so capable of unraveling all their work? Even if Bell wasn't playing the witch, Pie could let it be a deception, one he was in control of. Bell could protect her from the things he was stronger than, but Paimon, Great King of Hell, was not one of those things.

"And the detectives?" Pie asked.

"Merryweather sang the whole story to whoever would listen. I left when they let me. An ambulance took Josie to the hospital."

Pie's eyes tracked movement as Bell frowned, twitching in his seat. What kind of restraint had it taken the demon king to keep himself from following the little witch and healing her? Potentially dangerous as the situation was, it did prove entertaining.

"Well... you wouldn't be the first of us to get caught up with them," Pie said softly. Bell snorted. "And I'm not inclined to lead a mutiny and take your position. I'll keep my eye out."

Bell nodded and relaxed. Pie would toss Bell out on his ass if that was what needed doing for the mission, although he might play the card at the last second.

"Good luck," Pie said, as Bell pushed up from his seat at the garden table. "From what I've heard, human women are a powerful lot."

Bell's teeth gritted almost audibly, and he left the garden for the house. The cigarette was burnt out right down to the filter, stinging Pie's human skin where he'd forgotten about it. He dropped the butt in the ashtray and lit another.

Light flickered on in the corner of his eye, and Pie's stare shifted back across the garden to the carriage house on the other side of the fence. Slowly, carefully, Pie allowed a small amount of color to filter into his vision. He preferred to see in black and white and gray in the human world, cutting away some of the distraction and clutter. It was easier to focus, easier to mute the natural glitter of Earth and focus on the mission.

The curtains on the second story were sheer, in shades of orange and pink and green, mismatched and vibrant. Pie twisted the smoke in the air to frame the picture as a shadow stepped up to a window, pulling back the curtains. Dark curls bounced in every direction, and Pie smashed color back down, retreating to grays as Rosa Velasco stood in her bedroom window and stared back at him.

The green witch was vibrant even without color, and Pie played with his own curiosity on slow evenings. She had blue bottles in her kitchen windows, and multi-colored Christmas lights wrapping around her stair railings. He wondered what shades she came in but hadn't looked yet.

The witches were proving a complication in Sweet Pea. Now, with Bell compromised, the last thing they needed was for Pie to be distracted by his curiosity. He stubbed the cigarette in the ashtray and stood, leaving Rosa watching him retreat to the house from the view of her upstairs window.

22

A KING ON THE STREETS

"I mean honestly, *what* was that man thinking?" Mrs. Montgomery said, staring long enough at Josie from across the counter that Josie thought she might be seriously looking for an answer. "Well, I mean, we all know the vote was pinned to keep the park."

Josie hummed and nodded, eyeing the line from her counter out the front door of the bakery. At least no one looked impatient to get their pastry. Of course, that was because they were all here to tell Josie that they never, not for *one second,* doubted that she had nothing to do with the murders.

The news of Merryweather's confession spread like wildfire, not just through Sweet Pea but through all the surrounding towns, largely due to Bell's over enthusiastic magic on Merryweather, who spouted the confession to anyone who stepped within hearing distance. By the time the coven picked Josie up from the emergency room, the news had made it to everyone's ears. Merryweather had managed his goal in one fashion, his family name was now vividly painted in the community memory. Sweet Pea was only too happy to gobble up the equally sordid version of events, and Josie was now a 'local' darling.

"I think he was just looking forward to the money, honestly," Josie said. "What can I get for you today?"

"Oh, I am *sure* you're right," Mrs. Montgomery nodded. "Oh, I just don't know it all looks *so good*. And so reasonable too. Did you lower your prices, honey?"

She had not, although Josie thought now might be a good time to raise them. "Same as ever."

"Well I'll just have..." And then Mrs. Montogomery genuinely shocked the hell out of Josie with an order that was as long as the line to the counter.

What on earth had that woman said about her that she felt this guilty?

This is as good a way as any to take an apology, a voice murmured in her head. It sounded suspiciously like Bell.

To Mrs. Montgomery's credit, she didn't even bat her false eyelashes at the total, just took her pastry box with the world's corniest grin and leaned across the counter, lowering her voice in a conspiratorial manner. "Oh, and I just can't wait till tomorrow night." Then she giggled like a school girl and waddled her way out the door, bleach blonde curls bouncing.

Josie swallowed her startled laugh and served her next customer. So, Montgomery was coming to their Samhain circle. Well, alrighty then.

They'd decided, bundled up together as a coven in June's soft apartment, with bandages around Josie's freshly tended stomach, to go ahead and invite the town to the circle. Sure, they were proven innocent, but this couldn't hurt. The town had made an official Facebook event out of it, and Josie suspected their audience was about to be a lot bigger than June had planned for.

Josie served the line of customers that just seemed to keep growing, until for the first time in Josephine's Bakery history, she had to close early due to being sold out. It wasn't an entirely *good* feeling. She knew the reason they were there; to gawk or to absolve their guilt. There was a kind of satisfaction to it though. She prepped for the next day with the lights off and the kitchen door shut, and then locked up and walked down to Knots and Knittery.

June's wards tangled around her like a spider's web as she stepped inside, filmy and clinging against her skin.

"Hey," June greeted, the magic fading. "Everything okay?"

"Yeah! Yeah, I just sold out and got to close early, actually."

"Oh," June set down her knitting and started toward her purse on the shelf behind her desk. "I'll let you into the apartment, you probably want to rest."

"Actually. I was thinking... I think I'll go ahead and get back into my apartment," Josie said.

June paused, silver eyes wide and startled. "Are you sure?"

Josie had stayed with June for the week since Merryweather had broken in, and Josie had never felt a place that seemed safer or more protected than June's little apartment. It was a relief to be there, and surprisingly easy, even with her and June being so different. But she had work that needed doing, and situations that she had to stop avoiding.

"I'm sure," she said, nodding. "I need to get my altar back in order before I lose all the favor I had. And... I dunno. Need to feel safe in my space again, even if that takes some work. But I'll be borrowing some of your warding techniques!"

June smiled, cheeks pinking with pride, and she nodded.

"I'll make you some wall hangings too. Alright. I'm just down the road anyway. See you tomorrow for the circle."

"Hope you're ready for the crowds," Josie said, grinning as June stiffened in shock again. "Oh girl, yeah. We are the number one Halloween event in town tomorrow night. Get ready."

Josie thought she might even have caught a curse from June's lips as she headed for the door, but it was so quiet it could just as easily have been the click of knitting needles starting up again.

It was harder than she expected to bring herself to unlock the door up to her apartment. She stood at the bottom of the stairs, listening to silence until her heartbeat settled in her chest. The scent of ash was lingering on the air, and Josie frowned, hurrying up the stairs.

Instead of the wreckage she half expected to find, her apartment was... tidy. Bright. Possibly lacking a layer of dust that she hadn't gotten around to clearing away. When she walked down the hall and found the wall and floor completely clean of any trace of blood, and the familiar whiff of smoke stronger than usual, she realized what had happened. Bell had cleaned up her apartment for her, erasing the gory evidence.

The scars on her stomach gave a soft pang. They were healing now, itchy and scabbed over since Merryweather hadn't dug the knife in very deep, but they sometimes gave her a phantom feeling of Bell being nearby. She didn't really mind it.

Her fingers reached up to her lips in absent thought as she approached her bedroom. The memory of the kiss was always halfway present, trying to distract her from the real world and back to a moment full of confusion. Confusion and clarity. The attraction had been present from the beginning, of course. The *demand* to consume one another was a minor revelation for her.

Josie stopped in the doorway of her bedroom, breath held in her chest. The floor was pristine, not a hint of Merryweather's circle, and not a drop of her blood. Even more startling was her altar, everything clean and set to rights. Two teacups of rum sat out for her spirits, and candles flickered gently. There were cigars for Ghede Linto, flowers for Filomez, and strange foreign coins in surplus. It was so absurdly thoughtful that Josie wondered if she was wrong about it being Bell, if not for that very particular breed of smoke, something between cigarettes and pine.

She dropped her overnight bag on the floor by the door and crossed to her altar, kneeling in front of the arrangement and lighting a stick of incense on a candle.

"Glad to see someone's been here to take care of you," Josie said to her spirits. "Thank you, for making sure he heard that call. I really needed him."

The healing cuts on her skin tickled, the itch almost like a feather tracing over the lines. Josie hummed one of Mémés songs, trying to focus on her altar instead of the demon persistently at the back of her thoughts. She'd seen Bell around town in the past week, usually riding past her window on his motorcycle with the rest of his crew. She wasn't sure what he was planning next, or if the words he'd said to her before the kiss still held true.

She wanted to find out.

"I'm gonna do... a stupid thing," Josie whispered, focusing on Filomez's flower crowned figurine. "And if it's a really, really, *really* bad idea, I hope you think of a way to stop me."

Josie held her breath, waiting for the phone to ring or the candle to flare, or anything at all really that she might be able to divine as a stop signal. When nothing happened, not even a car honk from the street, Josie sighed and smiled. Well then, time to get to work.

———

JOSIE DIDN'T HAVE Imogen's archaic instruments so her chalice was a nice wine glass full of whiskey, and the surface where she'd traced Bell's sigil was a dry erase board. Her stomach might've worked just as well, but she wasn't sure since the marks were starting to heal. She set a clove cigarette burning in an old ashtray she kept her keys in, because it reminded her of the smell of him, and a black candle burning on a tea saucer. Three sprigs of rosemary were dipped into a small bud vase, cutting through the scent of smoke every time she passed them.

Her circle was perfectly round and took up every available inch of space of the open floor. Bell was a tall man and he'd probably be a taller demon, so Josie made it nice and roomy.

When everything was in place, she tugged at the ties of her robe around her waist. She was naked underneath and feeling highly self-conscious of the fact. She'd been naked underneath when they summoned Vinny too, and she hadn't thought twice about it. But of course, there'd been no chance of Vinny *seeing* what was underneath.

Josie sucked her bottom lip between her teeth—she could still feel the memory of Bell's bite there—and took in a deep breath. She didn't remember all the guttural syllables Imogen had recited, but since Bell had come with the simple sacrifice of her blood and his mark on her skin, she thought she could draw him out with a bit more ceremony.

Standing at the foot of the circle she raised her arms and raised her voice.

"Thee I invoke, Beleth, the bornless one," she began. "Thee who—"

But she stopped just as suddenly as the air in the circle shimmered and Bell stepped forward through nothing, silver shining in his black hair, and a smirk curling up his lips.

"You could've just called," he said.

"You didn't even let me get started," she said. "Don't you wanna know all the stuff I was gonna say about you?"

"Tell me now," Bell said, smirk turning to a grin.

Josie's heart flip-flopped in her chest as lines crinkled at the corner of his eyes. She really liked that smile, the surprised and giddy one all tucked under sarcasm.

She notched her hands at her waist and raised an eyebrow, droning through her list, "Who is a math nerd. Who could beat me at a board game, probably. Who likes chocolate and quiche." She smiled as he laughed, a whisper of a sound that made her shiver. "Who satisfies."

Bell's laugh turned to a purr. "What do you need, Josie?"

"You're making this awfully easy," Josie said, fingers fidgeting with the cuffs of her robe.

"Would you like me to resist you?" he asked, glancing around at the circle. "Your language needs work, certainly, but the offerings are fair. And I haven't agreed yet."

True. Right. Josie squared her shoulders and lifted her chin. "We're holding a circle tomorrow night, a protection spell for Sweet Pea. I want the magic to be strong. Strong enough to..."

"To stand up against me?" he asked, but his gaze hadn't lost the hint of a smile. "Are you asking what I think you're asking, Josie?"

Why couldn't she get the words out? Her heart was rioting in her chest as she stared back at him, imagined what might come next. Warmth flooded up her neck. "Now that I think about it, I shoulda just called. I feel weird summoning you and demanding this."

Bell stepped forward to the edge of the circle until they were only a handful of inches apart, the magic of the circle preventing him from touching her.

"Ask nicely," he said, grinning.

Which was just the right tease to make the words break free. "Beleth, would you consent to... work sex magic with me?" she said, nose wrinkling. Making sex magic? Having sex magic? Performing?

Bell bent, and Josie felt the wobble of power between them. He could crack the shell on her circle open if he wanted to. That was fine.

"Say, 'to my satisfaction,'" Bell murmured, his lips hovering just near hers.

"To my satisfaction," Josie breathed.

"I consent," he said, and then he stepped back, and Josie swayed forward as if he'd stolen all the oxygen between them. When he returned to the center he was naked, lean muscles flexing invitingly, and cock hanging between his thighs, dark and swelling slowly. His shoulders and thighs were embellished with strange, black tattoos—images between mathematical forms and constellations and twining knots.

"I was looking forward to undressing you," Josie said.

"Get inside this circle, Cupcake," Bell said, toes tapping against the floor in a gesture Josie found strangely innocent. "I can't reach you from here."

She toyed with the ties of her robe at her waist, enjoying the way his eyes fastened on the sight, his body tensing as she loosened them. The collar sagged open, and Josie felt a surge of power that had nothing to do with smoke or candles or spells as Bell's eyes took on a predatory glint. She let the ties drop, the folds of fabric hanging barely open, air sliding in against her skin.

"Come here," he growled, one hand sliding down to his stiffening length.

"Who's in charge, exactly?" she asked, head cocking.

"Let's find out," he said, eyebrows jumping and teeth flashing.

Josie shrugged the robe off, dropped it carefully away from the candles, and then stepped over the lines of the chalk circle, the whisper of smoke curling around her calves. She was already starting to get a little damp, the sight of Bell affecting her—all long lines and carved muscle, the way he completely blocked out the world with his broad shoulders as she stepped closer. Even more powerful were the colorful images passing through her head, all the possibilities of the next few moments. Who would win the hand for control?

When Bell's fingers cupped around her hips, tugging her against his chest, his cock pressing into her belly, Josie made up her mind. She pressed a kiss to the center of his chest where she could reach, teased her fingertips up his ribs, but when his hands slid down over her ass to grab at the backs of her thighs, she pressed her hands to the tops of his shoulders.

"No," she said, before he could lift her into his arms. His face was just above hers, and she took a brief, brushing kiss, leaning back as he chased her for more. "On your knees."

Bell's eyes flared with heat, those coals igniting in his dark stare, and he sank smoothly down in front of her. There was nothing like this, she decided, sinking her fingers into his thick hair as she pressed down on his shoulders until his mouth hovered in front of her sex.

"How does it work? Sex magic?" she asked, watching Bell's lips part as she tugged on a fistful of silky hair.

"Concentration. Focus on the goal," Bell said, leaning forward and nuzzling his chin against the tender lips of her pussy. Josie shivered, his stubble was surprisingly soft, and she wanted to let her eyes fall shut to savor the feeling. "I'll take care of that," he said. "I want you focused on this."

His hand at the back of her thigh pulled, and Josie gripped tighter to Bell as he balanced her on one foot, pulling her against his mouth. A soft praising sound fell from her throat as Bell's lips wrapped around her sensitive skin, pulling and pressing and licking as if he were kissing her mouth instead of her sex.

The light overhead flickered off, and Josie's eyes fell shut. Bell's hands were tight on her hips, and she was pretty sure she could've melted into a heap of pleasure and he'd have kept her fastened to his lips. The touch was slow and lazy, stealing her flavor and building arousal without driving her quickly there. He growled as he dipped his tongue inside her, and Josie shouted, clinging to him and rolling her hips into the touch.

"I should warn you," Josie said, voice gasping as Bell caught her clit at the tip of his tongue. "I'm not easily satisfied."

Bell hummed against her flesh, and Josie trembled. He curled one arm securely around her waist and then leaned back, his now free hand fitting between them to rub her, stirring up sparks of heat.

"I was counting on that, Cupcake. I don't plan on this ending quickly."

Josie blinked her eyes open, gazed down at Bell in the

new shadow and warm light of the room, a street lamp outside mimicking a full moon's blue cast on the floor.

"Do your worst, Mr. Bad News," Josie said, smiling.

Bell held her stare and moved his hand, spreading her open for a sucking kiss over her clit, his middle finger pressing inside of her. The contrasting pressure of the two sensations left Josie arching, rising up to her tiptoes as if Bell would let her escape the assault of pleasure. She raked her nails against his scalp, wrapped her other hand around the back of his neck, and praised whoever needed praising that demons didn't seem to need to breathe.

He fit another finger inside of her, the stretch a bite that left goosebumps breaking out over her skin, and then twisted them both, turning and crooking them forward. The slow dragging weight that had been growing in her center spread suddenly outwards, and Bell's arm clamped tight around her waist to keep her from falling as her legs curled up and a dark, electric ecstasy swallowed up every one of her senses.

Josie shivered and shook as the orgasm continued, flaring with every soft slurp of Bell's lips on her sex, and every slow plunge and pull of his fingers.

"Enough," she gasped, hoping he'd caught that magic since she'd definitely been unable to remember the goal of summoning him with his mouth doing the devil's work on her clit.

Bell released her with a wet pop, and it took Josie a full minute before the dizzy stars cleared from her vision and she could see the wet print around his mouth as he grinned. His fingers were still inside her, scissoring slightly, and he pulled her down his chest to wrap around his lap.

"I told you this wouldn't end quickly," he said, and then his hips rolled, cock nudging at her opening.

Josie caught her breath, and she dragged Bell forward, pulling roughly at his mouth and smiling as he growled into the kiss. She pushed his hand away from her cunt and poised herself over the blunt head of his cock, teasing the tip of him with her wet skin. Bell's hands danced up her back, cupping her head. He held her to him as he licked into her mouth, a steady purr emitting from his chest as they kissed. When Josie took him inside of her, just the first inch, the sound cut off abruptly. She bounced, sinking deeper, and opened her eyes to find his fixed on her face, their noses touching and gazes crossing slightly.

Her own flavor was on her lip, and Bell watched with rapt fascination as she licked it off. She released a slow sigh, body relaxing and fitting him further inside as his head bent, mouth hovering over hers.

"Are you focused?" she asked, raising an eyebrow.

Bell grinned. "A bit," he admitted. His hands stroked down her back and around her front, cupping her breasts in a warm, calloused touch that made Josie hum and start her rise and fall, feeling the perfect intrusion of Bell stretching her open.

She took another kiss, sucked on Bell's lips as he rocked into her until she'd taken him to the hilt. Their arms circled each other, mouths connecting with aimless tenderness. She leaned back, and Bell's eyes landed on her stomach, his hands running down and covering the wounds. Josie's breath hitched as the itching fizzled to nothing, and a tingling feather brush of power and heat covered the lines instead. When his hands parted, she had a shiny mark of his sigil remaining.

"I could heal that too, but I think I like it," he said. The corner of his mouth hitched, and a lock of silver and black hung over his eyes. Josie's heart stuttered in her chest, and she decided if she wanted the sigil gone, she could ask later.

Think of the circle, Josie, she reminded herself. Whatever they were doing now, it was for affection, not power. She pressed her palms to Bell's chest and pushed him away, and he only smiled, eyes skimming over her hotly as he let her guide him down to the floor. His legs stretched out beneath them, and Josie gave herself a moment to savor the picture of him under her, black and silver hair fanning out around his head, stomach muscles twitching as she shifted over him.

"Concentrate," Josie said, aiming for stern, and landing on breathless as she stared down at where they were joined, dragging herself slowly up his length.

When she slid down again, Bell hissed and she moaned. Heat flared at the end of her fingertips, prickling like a limb waking, and Josie repeated the action, swallowing hard as the sensation grew.

"Ride me," Bell growled beneath her, his heels planting on the floorboards and hands grasping around her ribs.

Josie took the order, thighs straining as she bucked and twisted over him, hips circling and grinding as he sank in fully. When a gasp and moan escaped, and Bell thrust up, teeth gritted and thumbs flicking at her tight nipples, Josie took that as her cue to vocalize her approval. The more she moaned, the wilder Bell became beneath her, eyes lighting up and teeth sharpening. She covered his hand on her breast with her own, and showed him how to pull and tweak at her nipple, harsher than he had been, rewarding him with a tight cry and clench of her pussy around his cock.

With every stroke between them, the power hovered thicker in the air until it was dense and cloying. Josie's breath was short, and the snap of her hips grew frantic, Bell answering her need with deep drives inside her. He gripped the back of her neck, holding her in place to take his pounding pace, and abandoned her breast to thumb clumsily over her clit. Josie rolled into the touch, their skin kissing wetly and voices harsh with gasps and grunts.

When she struggled to catch air, Josie planted her palms on Bell's chest and watched his tattoos shimmer under her fingers. She let him drive them to a slow cascading end as she released out a long, spiraling keen of pleasure. Bell threw them to the side at the last second, and the weight of him on top of her, thumb grinding against her clit, made Josie snap. She scratched down Bell's back, writhing beneath him as pleasure shattered through her, power blanketing around her until she thought she might suffocate. Bell snarled, mouth around her throat and hips kicking, and then he shuddered and sagged, clutching her tight to his chest.

His breath was damp and hot on her earlobe, and Josie twined her legs around his hips. He was still hard inside of her, and while physically she was *toast*, she realized there was something missing. She brushed her hands over his back and Bell trembled as the touch skimmed over his shoulder blades.

"Is that... is that where your wings were?" she asked. Bell nodded, pressing a wet kiss to the sharp corner of her jaw. "Does it hurt?"

"No," he rasped. "Feels sorta like...like if you passed your hand through bone."

That sounded like it would hurt, but who was she to judge? Josie moved her hands to his arms and turned her head to look at him. "I'm not satisfied, Mr. Bad News," she said. Which was a lie, in a way. She'd *never* been that satisfied with any sexual partner before. Damnit, she'd never been that sexually satisfied with *herself,* and Josie kind of prided herself on her personal physical understanding.

Bell nodded, nose nuzzling her cheek. "I know, Cupcake."

So Josie twisted in his hold, shivering at the slight shift of him inside of her, and reached back to smudge the edge of the chalk circle. As soon as it was broken, Bell surged up, Josie all twined around him as he walked directly to the bed. As far as Josie was concerned, Bell's best demonic skill was his ability to settle them gently onto her mattress on their sides without ever having to pull out of her.

What came next was slower, and softer, and somehow more secret than summoning a demon to her apartment for sex magic. Missionary was more or less out of the question —Bell was a mile taller than her—but he cradled her to him, arm under her neck, and her leg held over his hip as he struck a lazy rhythm inside of her.

"What's demonic birth control like?" Josie wondered at one point, when they'd stalled nearly to stopping in favor of finding sensitive spots. (Josie was ticklish behind her knees, but if approached correctly, the area could lead her almost directly to orgasm. Bell attached himself to her like a barnacle when she bit him on the throat, rutting and grunting and shuddering like a beast.)

"I am demonic birth control," Bell said. "Unless you summon me with a need for a litter of nephilim."

"Umm. I'm good," Josie said, uncertain of that word's meaning.

They separated briefly, so Bell could roll her onto her stomach and then determinedly wedged himself between her closed legs—a fit so tight inside, Josie lost her voice entirely. Bell didn't seem to have words either, but he nibbled kisses across her shoulders as he rocked inside her, until their hands were both fisted in the sheets around her head and their skin stuck with sweat. Josie came again, this time a syrupy, decadent, curling wave blanketing over her and leaving her limp. Bell released a bellowing groan against the back of her neck, a fizzle of heat running over Josie's skin in response. Maybe demonic cum was just magic? The thought made her smile as Bell slid off her back and to her side, pulling her after him and wrapping his arm around her chest.

We're fucking spooning, Josie thought in surprise, and then candles blinked out into darkness.

When she woke a handful of hours later, stomach roaring and reminding her she'd skipped dinner, Bell was gone.

Spooning is acceptable, but staying for breakfast is a step too far, Josie noted. That was alright. She didn't need him gloating about the fact that she was walking bow-legged after their marathon sex. When she rummaged through her kitchen and found half her stash of brownies missing, she gave up fighting her grin and let it stretch wide across her lips.

23 A SAMHAIN CIRCLE

The turnout to the Halloween circle in Merryweather Preserve was as big as Josie expected, and yet the crowd still somehow surprised her. Linda Love and Mrs. Montgomery and Mona Lin had organized a wide, pretty circle of solar lights to set a boundary between the coven and the observers. The woods were filling up with whispering locals, and Josie could tell by June's stricken, frozen look that she was regretting ever coming up with the idea.

Shortly before the circle was scheduled to begin, Josie looked up the hill and saw Imogen standing beneath a street lamp. She wore one of the oversized sweaters June knitted for her, and dark blue jeans, and Josie didn't know how to read the expression on the younger woman's face. Fear or sorrow or disgust. All of it combined but gentled. Just when Josie thought Imogen would turn and retreat to her cabin, the witch came stomping down from the top of the hill, slipping through the crowd of onlookers to weave her way to the coven.

"Will the spell still work with an audience like this?" Josie asked her.

Imogen shrugged. "We'll feel it if it doesn't catch." Then she took a second look at Josie with a keener stare. "Interesting choice. Bringing that magic with you for this work."

Josie almost choked on air as she realized what Imogen meant. She'd been walking around all day feeling *bloated* with magic after her sex with Bell, she should've realized a witch like Imogen would see it seeping out of her pores.

"Will it mess anything up?" Josie whispered.

"No," Imogen said, her gaze sort of sliding around Josie's edges. "He didn't corrupt it in any way. Surprising."

And then she drifted off before Josie could quiz her further.

The coven took positions at the four cardinal directions. Josie stood at the south end of the circle, holding a candle in her hands and representing fire. Rosa was opposite of her, representing earth with a wreath of lavender and rosemary and bright marigold in her hands. June was in the east corner, sticks of incense in each hand for air, and Imogen stood across from her sister holding a chalice of water.

June had written a script for them, a sincere and elegant prayer-like spell to call out as their magic wove together and laid over the town of Sweet Pea, but before the chant came the building of the circle. After working as a coven for five years, it was easy and silent work to catch each other's eyes, find a harmony of breathing together that would place them in sync with one another.

What Josie was less certain of was the influence of an audience. They usually worked in a close space together, hands connected. Here in the clearing of the preserve, they were spread wide apart, leaving room for the locals to stand outside and look in on them. Josie expected it to feel similar to delivering a school presentation, or having one of her old professors watch over her shoulder as she worked on a recipe.

Instead, as Josie found her breathing with her coven, she felt the connection of the circle traveling through the audience, not inside of them. The sensation was clearer than usual, probably because of her night with Bell, and Josie got faint reads off her coven—June's focus, Rosa's joy, Imogen's expectant edge. Behind her, Mona caught her breath softly, and Josie suspected the woman felt the gentle buzz of energy as well. *All* around the clearing, eyes and faces were lighting up with excitement, even in the silent prelude to the magic. Rosa beamed across the small bonfire at Josie, and a soft, dazed, satisfaction came around the circle from both Byrne sisters.

The four witches stepped forward together, inhaling and exhaling as one, their feet and hearts moving to the same rhythm as they raised their hands and called the corners.

"AND YOU KNOW," Linda Love continued to Josie, cheeks pink with soft embarrassment or the thrill of magic still raising the hairs on her arms. "If you need anything, you just let me and John know."

"Of course," Josie said, nodding and returning the fragile smile to Linda. She wouldn't call in the favor, but since it was actually an apology, that was alright.

Linda nodded and turned back to the larger, mingling crowd of locals, giggling as she joined her friends at the buffet table. Josie's chocolate croissants were long gone, and she was only a little miffed that she hadn't gotten to enjoy one herself. Rosa was somewhere in the crowd still, probably with Cornell and Thurman, and Josie had a feeling the

Byrne sisters had long since escaped the crush. The spell took, settling over Sweet Pea like a soft mist of good energy and safety, but even more so the townspeople had been made to feel a part of the ceremony. June was a good leader, even if she wasn't great with people.

Josie retreated from the lingering party slowly, wary of catching another well-wisher's attention. She was sure she'd shaken every local official's hand at least twice.

The woods were quiet as she found the path back to the entrance, and it occurred to her that Merryweather Preserve had a less than safe reputation now after three murders in less than a month. Maybe it was exhaustion, or maybe the spell they'd just cast was working, because the only thing Josie felt while alone in the dark on her way out of the woods was peace.

She reached the edge and found a familiar shadow waiting, broad shoulders and the curtain of dark hair, sitting sideways on his bike and staring down at his boots.

"Huh," she said, resisting the twitch of her smile as his head shot up on his shoulders. "Guess that anti-demon charm we just cast didn't take, did it?"

Bell's lips quirked. "Guess not."

Josie took soft shuffling steps up to where Bell was parked. "Oh well. What are you doing here?"

Bell's smile flickered, and his brow furrowed. "To be honest, Cupcake, I'm not quite sure. I'm still…"

"A demon?" Josie suggested, and Bell nodded gravely. "I know."

He still carried that warning air of smoke around him, that weighty aura that made his eyes glow dimly in the evening. She hadn't tamed him with one night, she knew that.

"You want a ride home?" he asked, dropping the subject and moving on into murky waters.

Josie wondered what the appropriate amount of 'playing it cool' was with your new demon lover? If he could be called that. It was only the once, and she'd *summoned* him for the deed, not that he seemed to mind.

"Think you can come up with a scenic route?" she asked, deciding that if he could deny the serious problems between them, so could she. She stepped up to him, and even with him perched on the seat of his bike, she still had to rise to her tiptoes to whisper in his ear. "I kinda like the feel of that machine running as I ride it."

Bell huffed a laugh and then shrugged out of his leather jacket, sliding it over her shoulders. It was huge on her, but Josie slid her arms into the warm sleeves and pushed the cuffs back as Bell shifted to straddle the seat and kick off the balance stand.

"Come on, Cupcake. You can show me the twists and turns around here," he said, and then he shifted as she climbed on behind him, and he leaned in to whisper in her ear. "I kinda like the way you wrap yourself around me while I drive."

Josie debated cancelling the bike ride in favor of heading back to her apartment like he'd suggested in the first place, but she didn't mind a little delayed gratification. And she really did love Bell's bike. Bell started the engine with a roar, and Josie made sure to hold on extra tight as they took off down the quiet neighborhood street.

EPILOGUE

The Byrne sisters stood in front of their parents grave at midnight on Halloween, arms entwined around each other. Moonlight was stunningly bright overhead, trimming the headstones in silver and weaving strange patterns of shadows on the ground. It was chillier there in the dark and out of the cover of the woods, and Imogen tucked in closer to her sister as June wrapped her large sweater around them both.

"The circle worked," June said.

Even the breeze was docile, teasing one of Imogen's wispy curls against June's nose. There were faint night songs around them, owls and crickets and the soft creak of a tree branch, but the whole world had gone drowsy. She'd worried when she first arrived at the preserve that the crowd would impede their work, but the locals had lent something to the magic that June hadn't expected. *Belief.*

"Did we over-do it?" June asked.

Imogen huffed, and it might have been a laugh. "There's no such thing as too much peace."

June hummed and combed her fingers through Imogen's

hair, ignoring the way her sister stiffened. "You didn't have to come with me. I know you don't... I don't mind coming alone."

"Protection spell or not, the demons are still in Sweet Pea. You shouldn't come out here by yourself," Imogen said.

In her chest, June's heart clenched painfully, somewhere between terrified of the future and touched that Imogen was thinking of her. Her throat squeezed, and her head went dizzy, and then Imogen's arms tightened around her waist and the dizzy spell subsided, June taking a quick gasp of breath. Ninety-nine percent of the time, June's thoughts were occupied by the worry of caring for her sister—their childhood was rancid, the years after worse, and Imogen barely bothered to aim for existence, let alone health most days—but every so often their roles reversed and Imogen grounded June. June suspected her sister was more adept at the role, because all it took was a touch or a look and her rising panic would settle under a wave of calm.

"Josie was stronger than usual tonight," June mentioned as her heart slowed in her chest. Imogen said nothing, and June resisted the urge to fidget.

"She went through a trauma. That can change your magic." Imogen said after a long pause.

It had changed theirs, more times than June cared to count. Imogen's withering spirit, their parents death... Brett and all the pain he'd served with him.

"I don't come here because I miss them," June whispered, holding tight to her sister as Imogen froze in place. "I think I come here... to remember what made they made me. The good parts." Few as those were.

"I would forget, if I could," Imogen said. She pulled herself free of June's arms and headed for the graveyard path. "Let the protection spell do its work, June. No more confronting demons."

June thought of the enormous Ash, filling her shop doorway with the sun behind him, and then buried the image. "I could say the same to you." June hadn't been the one summoning a demon years ago, not that she would throw it in Imogen's face now.

"Trust me, I plan on staying away from that trouble," Imogen said.

With Imogen's back to her, June brushed her fingers over the top of the wide headstone for her parents, cool dew gathering on her skin. What she hadn't told Imogen was that she came to the graves for the superstitious reassurance that their parents were still *there*. Still...resting.

Sure enough, the grave was peaceful, just like all of Sweet Pea for the moment.

June turned and followed her sister out of the graveyard.

ALSO BY KATHRYN MOON

COMPLETE READS

The Librarian's Coven Series

Written - Book 1

Warriors - Book 2

Scrivens - Book 3

Ancients - Book 4

Summerland Series

Summerland Stories, the complete collection plus bonus content

Standalones

Good Deeds

Command The Moon

Say Your Prayers - co-write with Crystal Ash

The Sweetverse

Baby + the Late Night Howlers

Lola & the Millionaires - Part One

Lola & the Millionaires - Part Two

Sol & Lune

Book 1

Book 2

Inheritance of Hunger Trilogy

The Queen's Line

The Princess's Chosen

The Kingdom's Crown

SERIES IN PROGRESS

Sweet Pea Mysteries

The Baker's Guide To Risky Rituals

The Knitter's Guide to Banishing Boyfriends

Tempting Monsters

A Lady of Rooksgrave Manor

ACKNOWLEDGMENTS

Thank you to:

KellieArts, my incredible cover designer.

Meghan Leigh Daigle, my precise proofreader.

The BetaQueens: Rachel, Helen, Jami, Jess, Kristina, and Ash.

My amazing Moongazers who cheer on each and every step!

All my writing babes, near and far, who inspire and motivate me.

My Momma Moon for loving me and my stories, and for running away to the mountains with me to celebrate this book.

ABOUT THE AUTHOR

Kathryn Moon is a country mouse who started dictating stories to her mother at an early age. The fascination with building new worlds and discovering the lives of the characters who grew in her head never faltered, and she graduated college with a fiction writing degree. She loves writing women were are strong in their vulnerability, romances that are as affectionate as they are challenging, and worlds that a reader sinks into and never wants to leave. When her hands aren't busy typing they're probably knitting sweaters or crimping pie crust in Ohio. She definitely believes in magic.

You can reach her on Facebook and at ohkathrynmoon@gmail.com or you can sign up for her newsletter!

www.ingramcontent.com/pod-product-compliance
Lightning Source LLC
Chambersburg PA
CBHW022125310726
48972CB00007B/2196